blue
rider
press

SWEET AND LOW

SWEET AND LOW

NICK WHITE

BLUE RIDER PRESS
New York

An imprint of Penguin Random House LLC
375 Hudson Street
New York, New York 10014

"The Lovers" was previously published in *The Literary Review,* Fall 2015
"Cottonmouth, Trapjaw, Water Moccasin" was previously published in *Third Coast,* Spring 2011
"These Heavenly Bodies" was previously published in *Indiana Review,* Winter 2013
"Sweet and Low" was previously published in *The Hopkins Review,* Summer 2014
"The Exaggerations" was previously published in *The Kenyon Review,* Summer 2013
"The Curator" was previously published on Amazon's *Day One*, August 2014
"The Last of His Kind" was previously published in *Guernica*, September 2015

Library of Congress Cataloging-in-Publication Data

Names: White, Nick, author.
Title: Sweet and low : stories / Nick White.
Description: New York : Blue Rider Press, an imprint of Penguin Random House, 2018.
Identifiers: LCCN 2017034368 | ISBN 9780399573651 (hardcover)
Classification: LCC PS3623.H578726 A6 2018 | DDC 813/.6—dc23
LC record available at https://lccn.loc.gov/2017034368
p. cm.

Printed in the United States of America
1 3 5 7 9 10 8 6 4 2

Book design by Gretchen Achilles

This is a work of fiction. Names, characters, places, and incidents either are the product of the author's imagination or are used fictitiously, and any resemblance to actual persons, living or dead, businesses, companies, events, or locales is entirely coincidental.

For Josh

PART I

HEAVENLY BODIES

PART II

THE EXAGGERATIONS

HEAVENLY BODIES

A thing is incredible, if ever, only after it is told—
returned to the world it came out of.

—EUDORA WELTY,
"No Place for You, My Love"

THE LOVERS

I.

The week before her flight, she records the twenty-fifth episode, this one about Arnie Greenlee. She's been avoiding the subject of Arnie since she started her podcast *Rosemary Talks* a few months after his death at the suggestion of her therapist, but now seems as good a time as any to mention him.

"While not a perfect man," she tells her listeners, "he was certainly an interesting one."

Arnie Greenlee was tall and rawboned, and sported the ugliest smile she'd ever seen. Big and beaverlike, his two front teeth jutted out from his full-lipped maw even when it was closed.

"Which wasn't often," she says in the dark studio. "My Arnie liked to talk."

The night Rosemary met him, at a sorority function in

the late 1970s, she spotted his teeth from across the room and assumed they were fake—those outlandish ones you buy at gas stations during Halloween. She went closer to investigate, which led to a lively conversation, the best one she'd had all semester, which led to horseback riding on his parents' farm in Starkville the following Sunday, which led—eventually—to matrimony.

"So I guess," she adds, "my whole life sort of turned on a pair of buck teeth."

Her bimonthly podcast normally lasts thirty minutes and typically, until now, shies away from the personal. In past episodes, she's interviewed local artists and celebrities, including a Miss Mississippi from the 1980s who came out as a lesbian years after her reign. She's given unconditional support to the last abortion clinic in the state and thoughtful reactions to movies of the day and detailed critiques of popular books. She's proud of what she has created all by herself, but she doesn't kid herself: The show isn't very popular, only a hundred or so listeners subscribe to it on iTunes. The journalism department—where she tapes the show at the small private college in Jackson—doesn't seem too concerned with ratings. They're happy, she gathers, to have someone like her (a woman, a person in the community) using their equipment. Her involvement allows them to check important boxes about outreach and diversity for elusive grants they are always applying for.

And she enjoys the talking—something she picked up from her years of living with Arnie. In the studio, a small five-by-eight box of a room, she kills the lights and speaks. "Into the void," she tells people, when they ask—which isn't often. Sometimes, like now, when she is recording a show, she likes to visualize her listeners: a small but dedicated bunch. Educated and practical, mostly Southerners with quasi liberal leanings. She thinks of them as loyal to the bone. And so they will forgive her digressions on Arnie this one time, indulgent as they are.

Summing up a person's life is a tough business. You're bound up by simple nouns and verbs. "He was a doctor," she says. "A father, an amateur golfer." She pauses to think. "He recycled."

They lived a quiet life in Jackson, running marathons, collecting old *Rolling Stone* magazines. He was the type of man who enjoyed taking care of people—his patients at the clinic, their daughter, and, of course, her. He gave back. A lifelong member of the Lions Club. Served two terms on the PTA at Jackson Prep. Some would argue—not Rosemary—that his generosity proved to be his undoing. His plane was bound for Ecuador when it went down somewhere over the Gulf of Mexico. He was doing volunteer work for Doctors Without Borders.

"That was Arnie," she says. "Always on the go. Until, that is, he was gone."

Rosemary hasn't been on a plane since the accident.

"Yet here I go"—her voice coming out tinny—"off into the friendly skies. Think of me, dear ones."

Here, she ends the show, hoping the goodwill of her invisible audience will carry her through her upcoming travels.

What she leaves out of the podcast is the reason for her trip. Her daughter's marriage is in crisis. An old story, from what she can gather: Her son-in-law has stepped out with a coworker, says he's confused, maybe in love; her daughter is bewildered, in shock. "Don't come," Amy e-mailed Rosemary after Rosemary had forwarded possible trip itineraries. "It's too crazy here," her daughter went on to say. Rosemary can read between the lines, however. The girl obviously needs her mother.

II.

Listening to *Rosemary Talks,* Hank can still picture him clearly: the man crouching on Hank's living-room floor and pricking Hank's finger, squeezing the blood out. He can see him dropping a copy of *How to Win Friends and Influence People* onto Hank's coffee table and telling Hank, in all seriousness, how this book had changed his life. "And not just my life," he said, in his laughing way. "Think Donna Reed, think Frank Sinatra."

Hank never read it, so maybe the doctor was being honest for once.

Dr. Arnie Greenlee had many lovers in his life. Most of them were men, but according to Arnie, Hank was the only patient he ever took to bed. (Hank has his doubts about this: Arnie, dear as he was, couldn't be trusted, particularly in matters of the heart.) Their affair started a couple of years before his death, but the first time they met, the last thing on Hank's mind was sex. For one thing, Arnie was much older than what Hank normally went for. For another, Hank thought he was dying.

He blames his parents for this. Their cliché and dated response to his coming out to them ("You're no son of ours!" they cried. "Sodomite!") sent him into an even more cliché tailspin of drug-fueled sexual encounters at truck-stop bathrooms along the Natchez Trace and in dingy motels off interstate exits toward Memphis. Hank, fucking with complete and glorious abandon, stuck his prick in places he wouldn't have normally put a big toe, and eventually, his behavior caught up to him. He lost weight—twenty, thirty pounds just fell off. He pissed all the time. His face became riven with acne sores.

He thought it would be easier seeing a doctor he didn't

know. He found Arnie's clinic on the Internet after a scattered search and made an appointment. Nodding, Dr. Greenlee listened to all of Hank's symptoms. Then one of his nurses took Hank's blood, ran some tests, and when the results came back the following week, he met with Hank in his big-windowed office, sucking on his big teeth. Hank found them suggestive, those teeth. They gave an otherwise plain appearance—pleated khakis, a red-checkered dress shirt, a pair of loafers—some much needed personality. Some bit of intrigue. If the doctor were smiling he would look roguish, much younger than the sprinklings of gray hair suggested. But he was not smiling. Instead, his face was devoid of all emotion, the professional look of doom.

"I got it, don't I? The bug," Hank said before Arnie could speak. "Oh, damn, oh, damnit."

Arnie laughed. "No," he told Hank. "But your blood sugar is unusually high."

Hank blinked, the information not computing.

Arnie clarified: "You're diabetic."

No word had ever before rung so beautifully in Hank's ears. *Diabetic*—it was magical. A line of poetry. As Arnie Greenlee rattled off how Hank was type 1 and needed insulin and should consider a healthy diet, Hank went somewhere else: He saw himself riding a bicycle through Jackson, without a helmet, legs akimbo, the sun on his back, not a care in the world. At some point during Arnie's spiel,

Hank—so grateful—leaned forward and kissed the man square on the lips, their teeth bumping together.

"I'm sorry," Hank said, thoroughly embarrassed with himself. He stood up to leave.

But Arnie placed a hand on Hank's shoulder. "I should come over," he said, "and cook for you."

"Cook for me?"

"I don't think you understand what's ahead of you. Your whole lifestyle will have to change."

"My lifestyle." Hank smiled. "My parents will be so pleased."

They kissed again. And, later that night, when Arnie dropped by Hank's apartment, he did cook for him. Hank would remember the meal—saucy chicken adobo with boiled asparagus. The spices, the heat from the skillet he rarely used, the way the asparagus sopped up the juices when the chicken was gone. "Stalks of flavor," Arnie called them. He would remember so much about that first evening: Arnie walking him through how to give himself a shot of insulin in the belly before dinner and how, two hours later (after he had fucked Hank), he ensured that Hank checked his blood glucose. Perhaps more romantic than it should have been: naked Arnie Greenlee gently holding Hank's ring finger in his large meaty palm as if he were proposing marriage while he carefully, tenderly, eked out droplets of Hank's sugary blood onto a thin test strip. When Hank's BG came back as 119, Arnie grinned ear to ear. *His teeth,* Hank thought. *Dear Lord, just look at them.* But Arnie seemed unashamed of his wrecked mouth. Proud even. And he did look roguish, Hank decided. Like a pirate only recently gone to seed.

Soon Hank found himself relaxing into this new relationship. Arnie, who Hank always wagered was one part golden retriever, had a way of causing Hank to relax about so many things. After they became lovers, he was convinced to give up refined sugar. Then he started recycling. By the time he realized Arnie had a wife, he was—to his great surprise—relaxed about that too. He had no big designs on the doctor: The man was a placeholder, a bridge from his younger days of indiscriminate sex with whomever fell into his bed to his budding desire for something steadier and (maybe) monogamous. But then Arnie got himself killed in a plane crash, and shit got complicated.

And now, as Hank listens to the wife's podcast, he closes his eyes and imagines the doctor at the moment of his demise. Midair, he's oblivious to the sound of engine trouble (even if there was such a thing) or those first few death rattles of turbulence. This is pure speculation, but giving into it makes Hank feel better about the situation somehow. He sees Arnie contained in his economy comfort seat, his face hidden behind a *SkyMall* magazine, looking at a glossy photograph of one of those braces you strap to your shoulders. He often talked of getting one. His posture had gotten so bad there at the end.

III.

At her gate nearly two hours before takeoff, Rosemary is seated in a puke-colored chair bolted to the floor in front of a large window overlooking the tarmac. It's sunny out, and she's coated in buttery light, the kind that cooks you to sleep. She dozes, dipping her head again and again, when here comes Arnie walking toward her, all cottony around his edges. He's wearing a brown polo and a pair of powder-blue chinos. He's slimmer than she remembers, and his eyes are deep green. So green. But, on second thought, she remembers, her Arnie had brown eyes.

She jumps awake.

"Sorry," the boy says, and steps back.

He's in his late twenties and looks nothing like Arnie. His teeth are perfect.

"I fell asleep," she says, and yawns. A feeling comes over her that perhaps she knows him. But no: This is wrong—it is *he* who seems to know *her.*

"I need to ask you . . . ask you something." His voice is soft—so soft that she has to lean forward in order to understand him, and that's when she notices it: trouble. She sees it all over his face. Her mind somersaults, working it out: probably not a terrorist (too preppy, too blond), definitely not a Hare Krishna (Did airports still have those?). But a con artist? An evangelical zealot worried about the fate of her eternal soul? Maybe. She rolls her hard-shell carry-on between them. What good it will do, she cannot say, but goddamnit, it makes her feel better.

"I'm listening," she says. "Shoot—I mean, um, speak."

He goes to, but the voice comes out slurred. He's dumbstruck and sways. Then his eyes roll back, and he topples to the ground at her feet. All very sudden: Maybe he's been drunk all along and she's just now noticed it. He was standing; now he's not. In the seconds that follow, she doesn't move. Stunned, she gazes about the airport. The people moving in front of her dash to the right and left, the clicking of their rolling suitcases trailing behind them. From somewhere above, an announcement blares, declaring the amounts of liquids allowed on board. Behind her, she feels the window vibrate with the roar of an airplane taking off.

What happens next, she cannot explain. Moving quickly, she stoops down and pilfers his pockets like a madwoman. All those years working at her husband's clinic as his receptionist before she quit to raise Amy take over; she's in autodrive, not sure what she's looking for until, at last, she finds it clipped to his belt, the size of a pager. An insulin pump.

"Sugar!" she calls out. "The boy's a diabetic!"

And my husband's a doctor, she wants to add, but doesn't. Arnie's dead, after all, and there's no power, she's learned, in widowhood.

Her shouting changes the atmosphere in the terminal. Almost immediately, everything slows. Travelers stop and gawk. Eventually, a fussy-looking airport official in a gray pantsuit and extravagant scarf trots over, saying something Rosemary cannot for the life of her understand, so she shoos the woman away.

"Honey, no," she says. "We've got to find him some glucose."

Now the airport attendant speaks briskly into her walkie-talkie.

Meanwhile, Rosemary returns to the boy's pants, searching. Arnie always told his diabetic patients to carry provisions with them for emergencies like this one. Maybe the boy's doctor made similar recommendations.

He's shaking all over and mumbling. She puts her ear to his lips, but the talk is nonsense.

"My watch, my watch," he says. But he isn't wearing one.

She places his lolling head in her lap and proceeds to go through his satchel, which is tangled about his stomach. He fights her on this, and so Rosemary has no other option: She slaps him. One quick pop on the cheek—she's repelled by how slick his skin feels, how amphibian. The slap works; he settles down.

She's vaguely aware of onlookers gathering around the two of them. Security guards muscle through, brandishing more walkie-talkies, repeating impressive-sounding codes.

Finally, she locates a cylinder of sugar tablets, grape flavored, in the outer pocket of his satchel. His mouth jerks open as she works one in.

"Chew," she tells him, and he does.

She gives him another, then another. After the fifth tablet, his shaking has calmed. Crumbles of purple sugar have collected in the corners of his mouth, and his wide face, blinking, is the face of a child just waking from a long nap.

They are hoisted to their feet and separated.

A small cart has appeared, and the guards usher the boy toward it, leaving her behind with the long-faced airport attendant. Suddenly, she comes to a conclusion. "I'm going with him," she says.

The words are strange in her mouth. But what's stranger, perhaps, is how no one objects. She's allowed to sidle up onto the cart beside the boy, whom she doesn't know from Adam. At the wheel of this contraption is an old Asian man who is all business, frowning as he spirits them through the airport in a flash of blinking lights. Along the way, the boy's head finds a home on Rosemary's shoulder. The faces they pass appear startled by the two of them. Rosemary lifts a hand to the audience and offers them, for no reason whatsoever, the queen's wave, her trip—at least for the moment—all but forgotten.

IV.

The doctor spoke of his wife with awe.

Hank had heard of her merits on many occasions. Arnie credited her with the success of his practice. She made friends with the right sort of people. Pencil thin, a wearer of flouncy blouses, she had an easy laugh, a comfortable way about her that Arnie enjoyed. Once, Hank asked him if he thought she knew, and he responded that he wasn't sure.

"It wouldn't surprise me," Arnie said.

Hank knew of couples like this. They were called white marriages, an arrangement more business than pleasure. The Greenlees were a good business, he had to admit. They lived in a big tan-colored house along the Ross Barnett Reservoir. Hank had driven by their place many times, straining his eyes to peer inside the large bay windows. Usually nothing to see.

In the year following Arnie's death, Hank continued to cruise by, noting how Arnie's place fell, little by little, into a state of disrepair. The garden in the backyard went back to nature, overrun by weeds, and the windows became tinted yellow with dust. Come March, the fountain in the front yard was infected with a splotchy mold. Hank was increasingly worried for her. It became a habit of his to follow her around town. Whenever he wasn't working, Hank trailed her like a private detective—to her therapist's at the university hospital, to the grocery store out on Lakeland Drive, to the gray building that housed the studio where she recorded her podcast. Why did he do this? He wasn't sure. It comforted him somehow, same as imagining the doctor on the doomed aircraft did.

The podcast he stumbled on accidentally, reading about it on her Facebook page. He listened to it regularly. And when she announced her flight plans, he panicked, bought a ticket to Albuquerque too, and followed her—like some obsessed fan—right on through security. The airport in Jackson was tiny, and she was remarkably easy to find. He had no formal plan. Plans were not his forte. And it made absolutely no sense: going up to her at the airport the way he did. Earlier in the morning, his blood sugar had been running astronomically high, so he'd pumped himself up with several units of insulin beforehand. He wasn't thinking clearly, but since when had that ever stopped him? He had no intention of telling the wife about his dalliances with Arnie—not if he could help it, that is. What he wanted from her was simple: his pocket watch. He had come up with a story to tell her about this lost object that was mostly true: Arnie was his doctor, he learned of Hank's broken watch—a family heirloom—and offered to pay for its repair as a—he always stumbled here—a friendship gift? But he never made it that far, but still, the watch. He must have it returned to him.

An old timepiece that once belonged to his grandfather, a veteran of World War II, it was his parents' last gift to him before they discovered his sexual predilections and cut him off. The pocket watch had tarnished over the years and hadn't worked since before he was born, but Hank had kept it on one of his bookshelves because he thought it was—at the very least—an interesting conversation piece when he was entertaining guests.

During one of his visits, Arnie had admired it. Supposedly, he knew a guy who could fix it. Hank told him not to worry about it, but next he looked, the watch was gone. And the gesture, frankly, had charmed him. Then, somehow, Hank forgot about it entirely until it was too late.

When he and Arnie last spoke, they argued. Hank had let it slip that he'd become friends with one of Arnie's past lovers—Arnie spoke often of them, so it was only natural Hank would become curious. He was a cute guy named Josiah, who had Andy Gibb–style hair and a prominent chin. He owned a bookstore Hank frequented. Arnie wanted to know if Hank and Josiah had been intimate, and Hank lied and told him they hadn't. A practiced liar, Arnie saw through it and stormed out of Hank's apartment, and the next week his body lay at the bottom of the Gulf.

It was a shocking way to end things. When Hank learned of the accident on television, he dialed Josiah at the bookstore, not knowing whom to call. "Impact," he told Josiah, babbling. "My god, the impact killed him."

"How's your sugar?" Josiah asked. "Have you checked it lately?"

Hank went over to Josiah's place that night, and they huddled close together on Josiah's den floor, like a couple of fretful cats, and watched whatever bits of news there were about the crash. Investigators were unsure of the cause, the TV told them; some speculated human error. Later in the evening, lying in bed next to Josiah, Hank at last remembered the watch. He awoke in a sweat. Surely the doctor didn't have the watch on him on the plane. Arnie was bad about following through, so odds were the family heirloom never made it to the jewelry store to be repaired and was still tucked away in some closet at his house on that goddamned reservoir.

Hank nudged Josiah in the back. "I need to talk to her."

Josiah rubbed his eyes, still waking up. "Who?"

"The wife—she needs to let me look for it."

Josiah said he was hysterical with grief. "Go back to bed."

But Hank was already putting his clothes on. Alone, he drove to the reservoir. It was a clear night, stars mirroring across the water. The windows at Arnie's house framed several silhouettes. Hank had never known the residence to be so crowded. Vehicles lined the driveway and the street, all neatly parked. He stopped his car at the end of the lane, debating his next move. He could very well slip into the house, find the pocket watch, and then exit with no one the wiser. A number of people had come to console the redoubtable Rosemary—who'd ever notice him? He pulled his car off the road. It was late September, and the air was cooler than it should have been, causing his skin to prickle. He got as far as the mailbox, which had *GREENLEE* scrawled across it in frilly cursive, before he doubled over and threw up.

The next day Josiah e-mailed him. In it, he explained to Hank how the pocket watch was not what he was after. "It's a symbol," Josiah wrote. "You are holding on to a symbol of a past that doesn't want you, and that is hard, I know. I think you miss your family—when was the last time you spoke with them?—and the absence of the watch is now more real than the watch in and of itself ever was. You are troubled by the negative space it left behind, it must glare at you, and now it's doubly significant because Arnie is gone."

Hank didn't respond. After all, Josiah had been an English major in college and thought that gave him the right to interpret everything.

V.

She doesn't telephone Amy until she's sitting in the hospital cafeteria sipping an unfortunate cup of coffee. Amy answers on the third ring. She sounds as if she's just woken up—all groggy and confused—and interrupts Rosemary several times as she explains the situation.

"So wait," Amy says. "You're not coming?"

Rosemary apologizes. "I've already missed my flight. Plus, the universe is obviously telling me to stay put."

"Oh, thank god!" Amy gives her an update on the marriage. Robert, Amy's husband—the adulterer—has moved out, taking with him only one suitcase, leaving behind his beloved PlayStation 3, which means, Amy concludes, that he's not really gone.

"You mean you don't want him to go?"

"Would you have kicked Daddy out?"

They both understand this is what the TV movies call a "low blow." Calmly, Rosemary changes the subject and mentions the boy. "His name is Hank," she says. "Heard him tell one of the EMTs."

"Who?"

Rosemary reminds her, adding, "And I think he may be a homosexual."

"Mother." Amy clucks her tongue and proceeds to inform Rosemary that using the term *homosexual* makes her sound Republican, and Rosemary, flustered, asks her daughter just what in the hell she should say, and Amy tells her people use *queer* now, and Rosemary says, "Well, in my day, honey, *that* word made you sound Republican."

At this, Amy laughs, but it's a haggard sound and Rosemary isn't heartened by it. She repeats the advice her therapist gave her about counteracting grief: "It's important, Amy," she says, "that you stick to routines."

Amy tells her she has to go. "I've got these e-mails to answer."

Which is code, Rosemary knows, for *I don't want to talk anymore.*

So they say their goodbyes.

The boy appears not long after. Sheepish, he approaches the table, his green eyes never quite meeting Rosemary's. She downs the last of her coffee, then asks him if he is ready, and he nods. The strangeness of the circumstance washes over her as she rises from the table. How he doesn't say thank you (not that he *needs* to) or much of anything, for that matter, as they walk back to her car. Which is fine. Lord knows, she didn't help him to feel good about herself. Still. Did he just assume she would give him a ride back to wherever? In his world, was it common for people to completely upend their travel plans to tend to him? She decides he must be an only child. Like her Amy, who would, no doubt, act similarly.

She's putting the key in the ignition when she remembers: "Oh, you said you needed to ask me something."

"Your podcast," he says, glaring at the dashboard. "I recognized you."

He's dodging and her antennas go up. Something was amiss.

"How'd you recognize me?"

And this question stymies him far longer than it should have. She realizes he's lying. Arnie may have always said she was the most naïve person in stocking feet, but she knows what she knows, and sometimes she knows it all too well.

"I heard you," he manages. "Your voice when you were going through security. And I remember you said something about your trip on your show, of course."

"Of course," Rosemary says. "How nice."

They sit in the hospital parking garage for a long time, silent, until she remembers that she's the one behind the steering wheel. "Why, yes," she says, and cranks.

On the drive back, she questions the boy further. Turns out, he works for the Department of Education. Something called psychometrics. Rosemary tells him it sounds as if he were measuring psychos, but Hank tells her he oversees the standardized testing of public high school students in

Mississippi. "So I guess you're half right," he says. He was headed out west. A conference. Not serious enough, however, that missing it will get him in any kind of trouble. As the boy talks, Rosemary gets comfortable with him. She wonders if maybe she misjudged him. Maybe he wasn't lying. Maybe that's just the impression he gives. It must be tough business being gay in Jackson. By the time they reach the exit for the airport (she's driving him back to his car), she gets the idea to invite him to dinner.

"Nothing special," she says. "Just steaks on a grill—very low carb."

The boy momentarily pales, but he assures her that he's okay. "Just been a long day," he says.

She gets him to agree to be at her house the following Wednesday at six o'clock sharp. Pulling the car into the drop-off lane at the airport, she turns on her flashers and unlocks the car doors.

"So it's settled," she says. "And you can even bring your boyfriend."

His eyes lock with hers for the first time. He squints.

Rosemary smiles weakly. "If you have one, that is."

He throws back his head, laughing. Like her daughter's, there's no heart in it. Only later, when she's back home, does she realize there'll be no dinner. They hadn't exchanged contact information; he has no idea where she lives.

VI.

After he gets home, Hank calls Josiah.

They haven't spoken since the e-mail, but Josiah doesn't seem surprised to hear from him. Hank confesses everything at once: following the wife, confronting her at the airport (What was he thinking?), having an attack of low blood sugar at the most inconvenient time. He finishes the recap by assuring Josiah that he's in therapy, which is a lie, and he fully expects Josiah to hang up on him. Instead, he asks, "Where are you?"

An hour later, they are sitting in the break room of the bookstore, a dimly lit little room with a mini fridge and a microwave and a dartboard with Ayn Rand's picture plastered across it. During their short dalliance in the weeks leading up to Arnie's demise, Josiah never took Hank back here.

"Like what you've done with the place," Hank says.

"Thank Arnie—he's the one who helped me buy it."

"This whole break room?" Hank places a hand over his chest. "Bless his poor combustible heart." He's laughing now, the same hard, dry laugh that came over him in Rosemary's car, except that this time it quickly turns into tears.

Josiah lets him cry for a few minutes before he asks, "So the dinner?"

"Not a chance. I can barely talk to her in public."

"Good. I think that's good."

Hank wipes his nose with a wad of paper towels. "What if it's still at a jewelers' somewhere in Jackson? Waiting for him to pick it up . . ."

"They'd have contacted Rosemary by now."

"And if he didn't give them his real name?"

Josiah takes his hand. "Wouldn't it be easier just to say the watch followed him down into the ocean even if it didn't?" Hank notices that the past year has not been kind to Josiah. He's gotten thicker around the middle, and the circles under his eyes have deepened. He wonders how he measures up in Josiah's eyes. The past year's been no picnic for him either.

Hank frowns. "Closure."

"Something like that."

They agree to meet the next week at a restaurant called the Cock of the Walk, a catfish house on the reservoir themed around an infamous keelboat captain from the Civil War. The restaurant sits across the way from the Greenlees' house, and they arrive in the afternoon when the water ripples in silver ribbons and the ducks are out. They find a table on the deck and sip tin mugs of sweet tea. As the sky turns pink, their skin takes on a salmon-colored hue. They almost look like teenagers.

Hank says, "I think about Rosemary more than I think about Arnie."

"Me too."

"I wonder if she was happy—*is* happy."

"She sounds pleasant enough on her podcast."

They throw some corn bread at the ducks, then Hank asks, "What if all of Arnie's lovers listen to her? What if we make up her core audience?"

"Whoa," Josiah says. "That would make her, like, the ultimate fag hag."

The waiter brings their ticket, and while Hank is calculating the tip, Josiah sets a small box on the table. Hank stops multiplying and glares.

"Relax. It's not an engagement ring." Josiah lifts the lid from the box and reveals a digital smartwatch, the kind with a touch screen. "It has all the bells and whistles," he tells Hank. "You can check your e-mail, your pulse rate, your blood pressure."

"Blood sugar?"

"I don't think so."

"Well—nothing's perfect." Hank tries the watch on. It does look good on him. "I'd be a fool to accept it—to think it solves all my problems." He turns his wrist, inspecting it. "But I'd be an even bigger fool if I didn't. It's stylish and I *do* need a watch."

Josiah follows him home. Once inside Hank's apartment, they undress each other slowly, leaving a trail of clothes behind them as they shuffle to Hank's bed. Their bodies are soft, but the room is dark and forgiving. During their lovemaking, Hank feels another person in the room. Ghost eyes watching them. He claws himself from the covers and sees a figure in the doorway. Rosemary, her mouth opening as if to speak. Then Josiah's mouth finds his, and Hank is taken back to the mattress. When he looks again, she's gone, was never there, and there's a finality to this absence that he can't quite understand. As it was with the watch and, of course, with Arnie.

VII.

How well can you know a person?

A question Rosemary's therapist puts to her now and then. But she thinks the better question is *Do you want to know a person?* Because, frankly, she believes it's overrated. She has this idea that some of us are really two people. The person we show the world and then the person we keep to ourselves. She considers telling her daughter this when Amy calls her later that night after the airport incident. Amy's been crying, and she's talking fast, the way she did as a little girl when fessing up to something. As it happens, Amy has been lying. Her husband was not the one who had the affair. She was.

"It just happened," she says.

And as she explains how, Rosemary's mind goes to Arnie and his many affairs. To his credit, though, she's never set eyes on a single woman he'd slept with. He was very tidy, Arnie was. They had come to an agreement after Amy's birth: no fuss, no muss. He never pressed the issue of sex with her, and she never questioned him on his activities outside the home.

Her therapist often asks her about their sex life. She supposes one day, sooner or later, she'll tell the nitty-gritty details instead of her usual response: "Fine." And she's positive the therapist (and everybody in the free world who has an opinion) will say their marriage was a sham. But she knows—and, more importantly, Arnie knew—they were happy. Only recently did it become in vogue to share everything with your partner, but Rosemary believes that way lies madness. Arnie, bless him, never inquired about her past, the *what* that made her the *who* she is now, and so why should it be anybody else's business?

Say, just for conversation, there once lived a girl who was one person—one complete person, not a person for the world and a person for herself. They were one and the same. Then, let's say, it's her first week at college, and a boy she trusted, a boy from her hometown even, pushed his way inside her bottom-floor dorm room while her roommate was out. Say he did things to her that split her in two. Right down the middle. Years later, this same girl met a boy who was sweet and unassuming and never curious about the other girl behind the girl, the one she hid so fiercely. He's satisfied with what she gives him. And, consequently, she's satisfied with what he gives her. It's enough.

Rosemary notices the phone has gone silent.

"Mother?" Amy says.

She tells her daughter, "You just can't ever tell about some people."

The next day she goes out for lunch and ends up driving by the Department of Education building, where Hank works. She recognizes his car in the lot and cruises past it and continues on with her business: lunch at a café, groceries at Kroger. Around five o'clock, she's in the neighborhood again and makes another pass by Hank's work. This time, he's in his car, backing out of his parking spot. She follows him. He takes her to his apartment, a nice duplex on Dogwood Drive. There's latticework, a deck.

She drives on, thinking.

At the airport, he mumbled something about a watch. Her brain makes some connections. A month or so after Arnie's death, she was in the bathroom cleaning out his cabinet. The shaving kit, the mouthwash. In the back, there was a cigar box full of doodads: baseball cards, an assortment of dusty marbles, an old tarnished pocket watch, the sort men used to wear in suit-coat pockets. If she remembers correctly, initials had been carved into the back of it, but she couldn't make them out, which frustrated her. The cards and the marbles were easy to give away. Not the watch, though—she held on to it, and now keeps it locked away inside her curio cabinet, folded inside a hymnal, hidden.

Home from following Hank, she retrieves the watch and holds it in the palm of her hand. It ticks. There are things in this world, she decides, you keep for no particular reason, the things you haven't yet found a language for.

The next week she returns to Hank's house in the afternoon when she's sure he'll be at work. She parks across the street and walks over. She ventures into the backyard, where there's a water hose rolled onto a plastic spool, a bed of half-dead petunias, some monkey grass.

Rosemary checks the doormat first. Nothing: too obvious. Then she explores the crawl space under the stairs leading to the back door, then around the storm drain, then the birdfeeder. Finally, she has some luck: On the stone walkway, there's a rock a shade darker than the rest. She checks it—bingo. One of those hollow plastic things; she taps it open and finds the house key. She jimmies open the door, and the apartment is very neat inside: the layout is an open-floor design where the kitchen looks out onto the living room. In the living room, a pair of bookshelves hugs the walls. She scans the titles, discovering some of them she's reviewed for her podcast and a few she's never heard of. She sees a favorite of Arnie's and pulls it out: *How to Win Friends and Influence People* by Dale Carnegie. Motes of dust cover it. When she opens it, the spine cracks and pops. On the title page, in a neat hand she recognizes, is the phrase: *Read it and weep. Love, Arnie.*

She sits on the couch in the dark living room and breathes. Dust is everywhere: on her arms, her clothes, her face. She sneezes; she can't seem to sneeze the dust away. Her nose may bleed if she's not careful. She's not really on the couch anymore but somewhere behind herself, watching the body sniffle. An hour passes. Then another. The evening comes on. Outside, car doors slam. She tells the body on the couch to leave, but it's as stiff as the furniture in the room, the hands placed calmly on the knees, the feet flat on the carpet. There are footsteps. There's the scrape of keys. The front door opens, and Hank stumbles in, followed by another who's maybe a little older. They don't see the woman on the couch as they shimmy out of their clothes. They traipse down the short hallway, devouring each other in kisses. Then they're in the bedroom, and she's at the doorway, watching the way their hands drag across each other's flesh, searching. Always searching. She wants to tell them it's no use. You'll never find what you're after. Hank leans up in the bed and looks at her, as if he's been expecting her all along, and she almost speaks, but he's soon overtaken by his lover's passion, or whatever you want to call it, and the moment passes.

COTTONMOUTH, TRAPJAW, WATER MOCCASIN

At first, Pete didn't notice the snake.

After he'd flipped the riding lawn mower, he blacked out and was pinned to the gully of the ditch. The sun was just below the trees when he started piddling in his yard. Now it simmered above him, burning away the last bits of the dewy cool he liked to work in. He was flat on his back, one leg crushed under the back end of the Cub Cadet—it had been an awkward fall—and his hip may have been broken too, which didn't bode well for a man of his years. His error had come in believing the mower could handle the steep incline at the end of his yard, the grassy plot by the oaks that stooped down into a sloppy half ditch he'd built to catch drainage. One minute he was upright, beginning to drip with sweat, enjoying the subtle art of cutting grass, and the next he was there in the ditch, blinking and struggling to catch his breath.

A Cub Cadet—he'd been told by the dealer—was the Cadillac of mowers. Pete had admired the honey-mustard sheen of the front hood, the way it hovered above his lawn like a spacecraft, the gentle tremor he felt as he held on to the steering wheel—all of it had lulled him into this mess. Now it sat on its side on top of him, dented and smoking, looking nothing like the glossy machine he'd bought a week ago.

He snatched open the hood. His hand ripped into the lawn mower's innards and yanked loose what toothlike parts he could reach, tossing them over his head. His wife, Doris, would call this a fit. Pete knew his anger, an old friend, and could feel it bubble up and eat through any amount of common sense he'd acquired since his youth. He wanted to gut the mower as if it were an animal. He wanted to pull apart its various mechanisms—the spark plug, the blade, the belt—and pile them above some kindling in his backyard and watch it all burn, watch the slow, greasy smoke ooze into the atmosphere.

But this was getting him nowhere. He was still trapped. Pete tried to move his leg from under the lawn mower by using his free one to lift the hull, but when he shifted his body to accomplish this, a sharp pain shot through his abdomen, forcing him to lie as still as possible. Normally, he could deal with hurt better than most: He was a retired railroad man and had suffered dislocated shoulders, cracked collarbones, and all manner of mashed toes and fingers. This pain was different, deeper than all the others, coming from—he reckoned—the very marrow of his leg bone. Pete felt his age in this pain and, for the first time, the fragility of his own existence.

Pete was quiet for nearly an hour, counting his breaths, waiting for the pain to pass, which it did, finally, in slow increments.

He yelled—one long bellow that came from his gut and silenced the whippoorwills. No one would hear him, he knew this much: He lived in a small single-wide far from town, Doris had been dead for nearly three years, and he'd run off his faggot of a son long before that. When he turned his head to spit, he saw the snake for the first time, its blackish body coiled tightly and shimmering like a puddle of oil.

The snake lifted its triangular head and hissed, the shock of white in its mouth telling Pete everything he needed to know. Cottonmouth, trapjaw, water moccasin—he knew it by all of its names. Back when he was a boy, his father would take him snake hunting at the river that ran by their house. With a machete in each hand, they'd cut through thick nets of honeysuckle, sumac, and kudzu along the bank, rooting out their nests. He was taught to swing his blade to catch the snake right below the head, cutting it off with one great swoosh of his arm. Pete knew the cottonmouth would strike just for the hell of it, that it didn't know how to retreat back to the overgrowth when you came after it like the rattlers and copperheads did, and that it would meet you where you were, refusing to be anything but predator.

Once, when he was grown and the days of hunting with his father were long over, he'd run across one and splayed it in half with the spade of his shovel, and its body had still twitched and curled forward toward him, unwilling, he had thought, to succumb to its fate. Pete had learned the secret about killing then—the joy that came with watching a thing die, watching for the last twitch and the silence that came to it and knowing you were the cause.

THE SNAKE UNBRAIDED its long body and glided closer to Pete, no more than a foot away. Its split tongue twittered in the air. The smell of gas settled quietly over him. He felt dizzy from the fumes and thought he might pass out again. He forced his eyes to stay open and kept them on the snake.

He dug his hands into the grass and dirt; he made balls of sod and threw them at the snake, but his aim was shaky. The snake was unmoved, and Pete hated it for its persistence, for the way it looked at him, almost as if it knew Pete. As many as he'd killed over the years, he'd never really looked at one before, studied the intricacies of each scale that hugged its muscular body, the same geometric patterns he'd seen on the quilts his grandmother would darn, its belly a light green, deepening in color and richness as the scales ran up its hard back. Rudy would have found something beautiful there, but his son was an idiot, prone to bouts of laziness and distraction.

When the boy was sixteen, he left home, said in a note to Doris that he was tired of Pete's beating on him all the time and thought he could fare better on his own. But Rudy was like that. Pete didn't fault him for his softness, but he did fault him for not having the good sense to know how to hide it. Each time he took a belt to him, Pete hoped to instill some meanness into the boy, one stroke after another.

The snake was taking its time, inspecting the ground carefully before it slunk forward. Its movements were slow, methodical, and it was so close to him now that he could smell the muddy river water and dark earth it must have hatched from, an odor altogether better than the gas. Pete wondered, briefly, if he'd killed any of this snake's kin in the past—there were so many snakes in his past, balls of them.

When they had finished on the river, his father would make him put the snake heads in a corn sack so they could show his sisters what work they'd done. He was lucky being a boy—his sisters, after their mother died, had to deal with things much worse than beatings. This usually happened late on summer weekends when his father was high on corn whiskey. His sisters slept in the room next to his, and on those nights, he could hear the terrible grunting coming through the walls. One time, when Pete was big enough to matter, he took up a kitchen knife and burst in on them with plans of murdering his father, but he, naked and unafraid, laughed as Pete shook the blade at him. He grabbed Pete by the collar and dragged him down the hall and threw him out the back door into the garden. There, his father jumped after him, swiping a cattail, breaking it cleanly from the ground. When it was over, Pete was all welts and bruises, and had enough venom welled up inside to carry him forward for sixty years.

PETE WONDERED what his father and son would think if they saw him now, half-dead under this hulk of metal, at the mercy of a snake. They would laugh. He knew they would. For different reasons, they would call this justice, would say how this served him right for not being what either of them thought he should be. The closer the snake came, the harder it was for Pete to breathe. He started to think about ways he could kill it using just his hands—if he could grab it in time, right behind the head, and squeeze, pinching off its air supply, or if he could bite it first, tear it apart the way a sow would.

"Come if you're coming," he said to the snake, and hoped his deep voice would scare it off. Instead, the snake seemed curious about the noise, slithering closer, head erect. Pete looked into its large round pupils and found them without depth, without emotion. The snake hissed, its curved fangs inches from his face, and went for his neck, and Pete felt its tongue fluttering against the soft contours of his throat. He felt the imprint of its head on top of his Adam's apple. For a moment, they breathed in tandem, pulse to pulse. It braved to skim across his neck, and Pete could feel each of its tiny ribs as it treaded across his skin, rubbing his flesh like sandpaper. Then it was over. The snake had left him.

He was alone, and the hours passed by slowly. Maybe the easier way out would've been to endure the snakebite: a quick, needled kiss, and then nothing left but his emptying out into blackness. If he did die here, it would be a slow, painful end—he saw it plainly: starvation, heatstroke. The ants would eat his face for breakfast, and the mailman would find what was left tomorrow afternoon. The local newspapers would do a story on him—"Man Found Dead in Front Yard"—that would drift into rumor, a sad story husbands would tell their wives at dinner. And his son would be called to come to identify his remains and would be glad at what he saw. Pete longed for the snake to return. He shut his eyes and imagined where it was now—behind him somewhere, perpetually moving, heading across the road to higher grass.

GATLINBURG

We heard about the bears almost from the moment we arrived in the mountains. First from the family staying in the condo next to ours. Then there was the chatty couple at the Dixie Stampede and later the old man on the Doppelmayr as we coasted up the side of Mount Harrison.

It happens every year, they told us, after the spring thaw. A wayward bear, still groggy from cave hibernation, wanders into someone's backyard, assaults a garbage can, and demolishes lawn furniture, before finally hulking away to the nearest water source.

"They're so dangerous," our waitress at the pancake house said, "and adorable too—it's really very confusing."

Our first night we peered out the second-story bedroom window at the conifers bristling in icy moonlight and the spaces of blue-black sky between them. No sign of wildlife anywhere: no feathered-owl dance, no opossum trundling through, no bear.

"Where have they all gone?" Reed said. He was a New Yorker; he had expectations.

"Dolly Parton," I said. "Maybe she collects them."

"I'd feel better if we saw one."

"A bear?"

"A bear."

I went to brush my teeth, and when I came back, he was still staring out the window. Our suitcases lay scattered about the floor, clothes exploding from them. I picked up a sock and threw it at him.

"Hey, you," I said. "They're not coming."

"Imagine just walking up on one. Eating or something. No fence to separate you. Just you and the bear, and each of you looking into the other's eyes." He paused. "Nature."

I turned out the lamp beside the bed and got under the covers. Soon, I felt his warm body beside mine, and we lay on our backs, breathing, not sleeping, knowing the other wasn't sleeping either.

"For the story alone," he said. "If we saw one."

"I'm already tired of bears."

"You're not taking this vacation seriously."

I leaned up. "Who takes a vacation seriously?"

But he didn't say. He had already turned over.

GATLINBURG

OUR TROUBLE HAD BEGUN long before Gatlinburg.

It started in Columbus, Ohio, the night we first met, at a Christmas party thrown by a mutual friend of ours. Both of us, the only two gay men at the party, had misread the invite, thinking the host had encouraged his guests to wear ugly sweaters, and we had arrived clad in hideous ruglike things: mine festooned with ribbons and cats, his a dense shag the color of vomit. "Perfect," I said, my first words to him. "We both look horrible." And he didn't laugh.

I guess I should have seen it then: trouble.

Or the night, sometime later, when he took me to the observatory on campus where he teaches astronomy. "Let me show you some things," he said, as I gazed through a large telescope, Reed standing behind me, his hands perched on my hips. He named the constellations I sighted: Canis Major and Minor, Cassiopeia, Taurus. He spoke of the magic of black holes and string theory, the sound of his voice a waterfall emptying onto smooth rock.

"Your accent," he said. "It comes on strong with certain words." He leaned in close. "I like it."

"You smell like butter."

"*Butter*," he repeated. "See? I can hear Mississippi in that word."

What followed came easily enough, as everything else did in those early days: using our coats to soften the floor of the observatory, undressing each other, folding our socks into our sneakers' sagging mouths. Beside us, an old spiral staircase leading up to the telescope room squeaked like a frenzy of bats as he worked himself inside me for the first time. The noise kept up for as long as we did: *So this, is this your life? So this, is this your life?* the staircase asked. Again the trouble, you see, even in the language of things we didn't care to listen to.

And afterward, that same night, back at his apartment—here too: We had showered and were huddled close to each other in his twin bed. He told me about his childhood riding the subway, hurtling underground from one place to another, Manhattan his backyard. He traced along the scar on my back, and said, "What's the story here?" and I said, "Oh, you know."

But he didn't, and I refused to elaborate.

We fell into something like love anyway, our bodies becoming familiar and, as it were, difficult to give up. The trip came about after almost a year of our trying to learn how to speak the other's language and failing, time and again, but still managing to be together. Parting ways seemed harder to do than whatever it was we were doing instead. The trip was a gift from Reed's mother, a successful real estate agent in Manhattan. A grateful client had offered her a couple of weeks in the Smoky Mountains as a thank-you for securing his mistress a reasonably priced apartment in Brooklyn.

"It's sure as shit not Colorado," she said. "But free is free. And yours if you want it."

Initially, I didn't want it. I'd not stepped foot in the South since I came out to my family in Vicksburg. The Smoky Mountains aren't technically the South, I know, but to me, it was close enough. Reed said the change in scenery would do us good. "Please," he said. "We need this." He looked at me, and I saw the truth: *He* needed this.

THE DAY AFTER WE ARRIVED, we drove through Great Smoky Mountains National Park, down trails just wide enough for my hatchback. Around lunchtime, we parked beside other vehicles along the roadside and followed a footpath to a small wooden cabin half hidden in a cranny of sumac and sunflowers.

Families and hikers milled about in the tall grass, eating Tupperwared lunches, making small talk. The cabin itself was shabby but clean. Well-kept. In front of it, an important-looking sign was planted in the ground, detailing how the cabin had once served as a schoolhouse, educating the mountain children in one large room with only a small fireplace to keep them warm during wintertime.

The inside smelled of black pepper and pencil shavings.

No furniture to speak of. Just a scuffed-up plywood floor, notched walls, a forgotten hearth. Clear light fell from one of the open doorways, electrifying the dust motes swimming in the air. Reed stood in the doorway, his hair made fluorescent, his shoulders glowing. He stepped out onto the back porch, not hearing me when I said his name. It echoed back to me from the high-flung ceiling: *Reed*.

I said mine then, and the old room cupped my voice and sent it back to me as before, as someone else's.

I said, "Motherfucker," and was pleased with how that sounded too, the treble of it: "Motherfucker, motherfucker, motherfucker."

WE WERE SITTING ON the back steps of the cabin sharing a granola bar when a band of rowdy children in overlarge Dollywood T-shirts came galloping through. A flurry of footsteps, great hoops of laughter. They burst onto the back porch and leaped over and around us, then circled back to do it all over again.

"Wildlife," I said.

They came through again. And once around the corner, they shouted to one another. "Got you!" a girl screamed. "I've got you now!"

Reed shut his eyes as he chewed the last of the granola.

"Does it remind you of home?" he said.

"The kids?"

"I mean everything." He gestured to the weeds, the scrub of trees and bushes three feet to our left. "The people, the land."

"I'm from Vicksburg. There are no mountains in Vicksburg."

He knew that, but it meant nothing to him, or it didn't seem to, which struck me with a pang of sadness.

"So what you're saying is," he said, "same church, different pew."

SOMETIME LATER, a park ranger came out of the thicket brandishing a megaphone.

"Attention," she called, the loudspeaker crackling her voice.

Everyone froze, even the children.

Very calmly, the park ranger asked us to return to our vehicles.

"A bear has been tracked into the vicinity," she added. "A large sow."

Reed rose from the steps. "Goddamn," he said, and rushed off toward her. When I reached them, they were already in a full-throttled conversation.

"You can't predict what any wild animal might do," she was saying, all too happy to talk bear. "This one's been acting scary for some time now. Ever since her cub got mowed down by a Camry a week back. Damn thing went rogue."

"Rogue?" Reed said. "How radical."

She told us the animal would most likely have to be put down. "Mama bears hold grudges," she said. "Won't do for her to run up on someone."

All of a sudden, the park ranger's walkie-talkie buzzed.

"Okay," she said into it. "Over."

There was more static, a voice, a command.

"Will do," she said, her face serious. "Over." She smiled at us, her cheeks large and shiny. "Like I said: unpredictable. Appears she's gone another way."

ON OUR WAY BACK to the car, Reed said, "We were close. Damn close."

I said, "Too close."

It was almost evening, and sunlight lay chandeliered in the treetops. A ruddy haze fell over us, tinting everything sepia. Bone-colored rock jutted up from the earth, and the Fraser firs were so green, they looked like gaudy cartoons of themselves. We left the trail to inspect a moss-laden fir he'd spotted and claimed was very old. "It could predate European settlement." He placed his hand on the crimpy moss, then I did.

"Feel that?" he said. "The tree pulse?"

"Nope," I said. "I have to pee."

Behind us, somewhere, something moved. Heavy footfalls. A shuffling.

"The wind," Reed said.

We hurried back on the trail, not looking behind us.

"Vindictive bears," I said, huffing as we walked.

Again, there came the noise. We picked up our pace, thinking the same thing, the only thing. The bear was coming for us. It happened a third time, the noise, and we were sent running down the trail at full tilt.

We sidestepped the parked cars as we came upon them, and once inside our own, we slammed the doors shut, locking them. Heaving, I cranked the hatchback, turned up the AC. Cold blasts of air hit our wet faces. Reed looked down at his crotch; he was pale, shaking.

"You see him?"

"Who? A bear?" I looked around.

"No, the man in the truck."

"Here." I shifted my air vent toward him. "Cool down."

He slapped the vent closed. "You are not hearing me, Eric." He pointed to the Dodge Ram parked a few yards up from us. "Him—you didn't see him?"

I told him I hadn't. Which only seemed to make him more red-faced. Slowly, he told me what he'd seen. As we were loping toward the car, the man in a truck we passed had fashioned his hand into the shape of a pistol and pretended to knock us off one at a time. At least this was what Reed had seen. "He was smiling about it too," Reed said. "Jesus, it looked like his son was in the cab with him laughing about it."

"Why?" I said. "How would he know?"

"Two grown men don't normally hold hands while they run," he said.

"Oh." I had no memory of our holding hands and this was a shock. "Maybe you misunderstood."

"*Maybe you misunderstood,*" he said, mimicking my accent.

I placed a hand on his leg, but he wouldn't let it stay there long. He guided it back to the steering wheel. "Drive," he said.

Meanwhile, the truck had already vanished. Gone quietly back down the mountain.

REED'S MOTHER PHONED my cell back at the condo while he was in the shower.

"What happened?" she asked. Something was wrong, she told me, because Reed had stopped responding to her texts. I went outside on the balcony and slid the door closed behind me. I filled her in about the man in the truck.

"Of course," she said. "I should have known."

"Nothing else happened. We're okay." I wanted to say how I thought he was overreacting, but I didn't.

"But you're from there," she said, almost as if she'd read my mind. "Sweetheart, you're used to it."

She'd been throwing a rooftop party when Reed took me to meet her for the first time. We lived in Ohio but were spending a weekend in New York. For the entire night, she trucked me around to all her guests, showing me off like an artifact. "This is Eric," she had said. "Reed's friend. He's from Mississippi—isn't that adorable? Just wait till you hear him speak."

She was now insisting she fly us to New York.

"Tonight," she said.

"I'll ask him," I said. I heard the shower cut off and asked her if she'd like to speak to him.

"Oh, no! I don't want to bother. You know how he can be. By the way, how are things—between you two, I mean. Any better?"

"Slowly but surely."

"Good! I'm keeping my fingers crossed you come back renewed—is that the right word? Renewed?"

"I don't know."

"Okay! Off to dinner! Let me know if you need rescuing."

The line went dead.

Reed was wearing a towel around his shoulders when

he came out of the bathroom. He was thirty-five, almost a decade older than I was. Still, he had the better body. A tight waist, a well-shaped chest. I had fallen in love with his body a little at a time. Starting, I think, with his toenails, how well he kept them trimmed. Then his eyes, his shoulders. The rest of him followed, even the less glamorous parts: the bald spot, the gray tooth, the ratty tuft of hair trailing down his back.

"Hey, sailor," I said, lounging on the bed. "Want to get drunk, fuck around?"

We locked eyes in the mirror as he rubbed lotion into his neck.

"You and Mother have a good chat?"

"She tried calling you." I told him about her offer to fly us to New York.

"How can we?" He slipped on underwear. Adjusted the crotch. "When I've not seen my bear yet."

I rolled over, burying my face in the comforter.

He cut on the blow-dryer, and suddenly I was very tired and, somehow, dozed off.

I woke up a few hours later to find him sitting in a chair in front of the window.

"You're obsessed," I told him. "You know that."

"Do you think people know? Generally speaking."

"What people?"

"Anyone. The general public. Residents of Gatlinburg.

The man in the truck. If you hadn't grabbed my hand, would he have known?"

"So I grabbed your hand?"

"I just mean it seems easier for you to take . . . what happened."

"It upsets me too." But that wasn't entirely true. Really, I was more alarmed we'd been holding hands without my realizing it. And the more I thought about *that*, the more wrong it became.

He came to bed, sat cross-legged on top of the covers so our bodies barely touched, the palm of his foot resting on my kneecap.

"Eric?"

"I'm here."

He turned on the lights.

"Why don't you ever talk about it?"

"It?"

"The stuff that happened when you were younger."

"The stuff."

"The scar," he said, and fiddled with a loose thread on the bedsheet.

I felt it then, my scar, blazing down my lower back, roughly the shape of California, so easy to forget except when it wasn't.

Reed was looking at me, waiting, his mouth hanging open.

"Stop gawking," I finally said, and laughed a little. "I'm not a bear."

"Okay. You're right. Okay." He was nodding as he turned the lights back off and settled onto his side of the bed.

I lay on my back, thinking. We are running, the two of us, the sun blazing. One hand reaching for the other's.

"And for the record," I added in the dark. "You grabbed my hand."

OUR LAST NIGHT in the mountains, we took the ski lift over Gatlinburg to a little resort area on the bluff above the city. At the top, our ears popped, and we ambled aimlessly in the streets before spotting a store called Three Bears.

"Oh, we have to," Reed said.

We paid three dollars apiece and were escorted by one of the staffers to the third floor of the store where, behind a sheet of plexiglass, slept three skinny bears. Their tangled bodies were one large bundle of matted fur that undulated.

"Wow," Reed said. "Here they are."

"Yep, in all their glory."

He knocked on the glass; nothing happened.

"This is, you know, depressing," he said. "I think I should feel depressed."

"Do you, though, feel depressed?"

He dragged a finger across the glass. "No," he said. "Something is missing."

Afterward, we sledded on a long plastic tube down the side of the bluff. At the end, one of the attendants told us it was much faster in the winter. "You'll have to come back then," he said.

Reed smiled at him, and said, "Probably not."

He wanted to buy something for his mother, so we stopped at a gift shop on the way back to the car. Every gift shop in Gatlinburg, it seems, has a specialty. Some claimed the best fudge; others touted the finest pottery. The one we found ourselves in held the market on snow globes. Glistening orbs on every shelf, each one capturing a rustic scene: snow-laden rooftops, various animals with stoic stares, pancake houses. I made my way to the discount table in the back, where there sat a large one featuring a heavyset woman inside, buttoned in flannel, a hatchet in her hand. Behind her, a felled tree the size of a cigarette. I picked up the snow globe and shook it, the snowy confetti inside coating everything in a brief blizzard. *Defiant Pioneer Woman*, it was called. Something about it, I don't know what. I returned it to the table, shaking, a lump lodged in my throat.

"Faggot," I said.

At the front of the store, someone screamed. Glass shattered.

I heard Reed's voice then, shouting.

By the time I arrived, the fight had already been broken up. Reed was pinned against a counter by a large man with bulging eyes, a plastic bucket of metal washers had turned over and were scattered at their feet. There was another man prone on the floor, clutching his nose. Blood oozed between his fingers. A crowd of onlookers had gathered.

"You simmer now," the man holding Reed was saying. "Just you simmer some."

Reed's eyes found mine. "That's him," he told me. "The man."

A boy was crouching beside the man on the floor now. The boy touched the blood leaking down the man's face. "Wow," the boy said, examining the tackiness on his fingers. The man, presumably the boy's father, wore a lime-green polo and had whiskers in his ears. He looked bewildered, frightened. A woman helped him up from the floor, maybe his wife, and took him to another part of the store, out of sight.

Only then did the large man release Reed. "I don't want any more trouble from you," he said to Reed. I had moved beside him and was touching his wrist.

An elderly woman appeared behind the cash register, toting a broom. "You boys might want to use the exit," she said, and so we did.

REED DIDN'T SPEAK UNTIL we were in the parking lot, an open square of concrete poorly lit and alive with the sound of crickets.

"That was him," he said. "The fucker. That was him."

"Okay."

"You know it was." He kicked my car's fender.

"Careful," I said. "My car's had a hard life."

"Give me the keys."

I scratched my shoulder. "You need to calm down."

Then came his fist, slicing past my face. I shoved him against the trunk, and we were at each other like animals, falling to the ground, gravel snapping in our ears. We snatched hair, raked our nails against whatever exposed skin we could find. He put a kneecap in the small of my back; I elbowed his ear. We bled and spat and cried out together, almost in unison—a terrible sort of intimacy, maybe the sort he'd been longing for this whole time. He straddled my shoulders, locked me to the ground. He panted.

"You don't know anything," I said.

He covered my mouth with his own, the salty taste of him; I bit his lip, drawing more blood. We pulled apart, both of us shaking between the parked cars. Now other people were in the parking lot, we realized. We heard them. Footsteps. Doors slammed shut; an engine turned. There was a flash of headlights. We hid behind the hatchback until the car was gone, and then we slid into the back seat. Reed shoved my pants down and pushed himself in. It didn't take long for him to finish, and while he was still inside me, recovering, I told him about the scar.

"My cousins," I said. "Battery acid."

"What?" he said. Then, remembering: "Oh."

I pushed my face into the seat cushion, wishing for his hand to find the back of my skull and hold me there until the urge to scream had left. Instead he lifted my shirt and put his lips, briefly, against the mark on my back.

In this way, we said our goodbyes.

THESE HEAVENLY BODIES

That was the summer Benjamin was so thin he barely cast a shadow, the summer he pedaled his clunky one-speed everywhere: around the dusty town square, across Turtle Bridge, down to Meryl Creek; the same slow-moving, bone-weary summer after his mother died and his father stopped preaching and his aunt Beatrice from Biloxi stayed on after the funeral until "things settled down," she said, which meant, he knew, until his father pulled himself out of his grief—that summer, which was so different from any other in his life so far, was also the summer of the Cade twins. They were new to town, and at first he knew very little about them, only what he heard from Aunt Beatrice, who mentioned them from time to time while talking with one of her girlfriends on the phone when he and his father ate dinner, silently, at the kitchen table nearby. "Their mother was a hippie. Said she did so many drugs her eyes never set right in her head. Poor things—was the drugs that made them that way, I bet." Or: "They're staying with their aunt for the summer—that rich lady pharmacist that works at Eckerd's, the one that never married, the one people say is—you know." Or: "A tragedy. I've not seen them yet with my own two eyes, but I'd cry every day if that was one of mine like that—all mangled together. An affliction."

Affliction—the word gave him pause, made him look up from his plate of Hamburger Helper and corn bread, past his father, who appeared to be reading something cradled in his lap, and directly at his aunt. She was twirling the phone cord around her wrist, listening to the person speaking on the other end of the line. She had just returned from Big Suzi's Hairport, and her hair was freshly dyed—midnight black—and relentlessly teased, forming a dark cottony helmet above her ears. His mother had once told him that Aunt Beatrice wanted to look like Kitty Wells, but Benjamin didn't know who that was, so he could only guess that this woman was his aunt's idea of beautiful.

When their eyes met, she took the phone from her ear and hooked it onto her shoulder. "Need something, sweet pea?" she said. He shook his head. She went back to talking, soon forgetting that he or his father were there, which he didn't mind. She would talk and talk well into the night, long after he had gone to bed. Some nights, the stout sound of her laughter coming from the kitchen would wake him. Jarred from his sleep, he'd lie in his dark room on his hard mattress, breathless and not quite himself—not yet remembering all the ways in which his life was no longer the same—and believe, for an instant, that the muffled female voice down the hall was his mother's. *No, stupid,* he'd tell himself, and rub his eyebrows. *Get a fucking grip.* But on that night, he didn't drift off to sleep until after his aunt had turned in. He tossed from one side of the bed to the other, thinking about *affliction* and the Cade sisters.

The word had biblical implications; perhaps he'd read it somewhere in the Old Testament. Back when his father had still been a preacher at Second Baptist, he made it a point not to use such words (he was never the fire-and-brimstone type, preferring, instead, to keep his sermons intellectual—so intellectual, in fact, that Benjamin would ask his mother to explain parts of them afterward). The word—he decided, as he kicked his covers off—had a kind of spit to it, an acidity that he resented on the twins' behalf. He felt this way partly because words had also been thrown around about him this past year—*troubled, angry, defiant, temperamental*—with the same sort of carelessness that he'd witnessed from his aunt. But, to be fair, he had deserved it.

Last year, in seventh grade, he'd been in three all-out

fights with older boys, and although he hadn't won a single match, he had learned to appreciate the pleasure that came from hitting and even from being hit. The first fight was in October, not long after his mother's wreck, and he had been so angry that he hadn't felt any of the blows that landed on his face. It was only later, when he was in the teacher's lounge being cleaned up by one of the custodians, that he realized his nose was bleeding and his left eye was swelling shut. After the third fight, which resulted in a table in his homeroom being toppled and a trash can severely dented, the principal had suspended him for a week. Before school let out for the summer, he'd called Benjamin into his office for a talk. "I hope you take this summer to think about your future," he'd told him. "You will be in eighth grade next year. That means something. What would your mother say about how you've behaved?"

The question had shaken him. He thought it foolish to wonder about what the dead think: If all the evangelicals were right, she was probably living it up in heaven and didn't (he hoped, at least) have time to worry herself with what she had left behind. And if death is the end, like going to sleep and not dreaming, then that was fine with him too, perhaps even preferable, because then she definitely wouldn't see how bad her son had become. In addition to the fighting, there were other charges against him: He had skipped a whole month of classes—the month after she'd died—wandering up and down the railroad tracks, leaving pennies and dimes to be flattened by the huffing freight trains. His grades were dismal; and he'd taken to bullying some of his classmates, the ones weaker than he, particularly the nervous fat kids with bodies built for ridicule. He ached to strike them again and again. He was small but wiry, capable of fast bursts of anger that surprised even himself.

Once, a large red-faced boy named C. J. Montgomery accidently squirted ketchup on Benjamin's shirt, and Benjamin, acting so fast that he wasn't quite sure what he was doing until it was over, took a wad of napkins that he'd used to clean the stain and shoved it into the boy's acned face. "Eat it, cocksucker," he'd yelled, his heart hammering against his chest. "Eat it like I ate your mother last night." The Benjamin he'd become had stumbled onto a secret no one liked to talk about: Being bad felt good, made all his other emotions—sadness, self-pity, worry—melt away. Aunt Beatrice kept most of his "behavioral problems" from his father. "Wouldn't do him any good to know this," she'd say each time after he'd come home with a note. It was she, without his father having the slightest inkling, who met with the principal time and again to discuss him.

In the darkness of his room, he found himself titillated by the thought of the sisters, and the mystery of them, and their mother who had condemned them. Drugs? Sex? Both? Was there something worse than drugs and sex that he didn't know about? They were, no doubt, troubled girls. Like him. Carefully, he slid the brim of his boxers to his knees and spit into the palm of his hand. He tried to think of what else his aunt had said about them so he could conjure a better image in his mind—"mangled together," "a tragedy"—but none of it made any sense, none of it pulled the sisters from the shadows of his consciousness. Nevertheless, he managed somehow, and soon he was coming. Then he turned over onto his side, straddled the covers. Sleep found him at last.

AFTER THAT NIGHT, he didn't think about the Cade sisters until two weeks later when he was at Lucy Gatesmith's birthday party at the Briarwood Country Club. Lucy was a year older, and the only person from his school he kept up with during the summer months. They took a beginning drawing class together that met twice a week—his mother, an artist herself, had forced him into taking the class, and his aunt had refused to let him stop for the summer, thinking, he figured, that art might calm him down some. During their time together, alone with Mr. Tuttleworth in his studio house, Lucy Gatesmith had developed feelings for Benjamin; he could tell by the way she spoke to him, all half-lidded and thick-tongued, as if she were speaking to someone standing behind him who was much taller, which he found both annoying and unnerving.

He pedaled the two miles to the country club, arriving all sweaty and ready to swim. In fact, the only reason he had gone to Lucy's party in the first place was so he could swim in the club's Olympic-size outdoor pool. He was disappointed to find that he was the only boy at the party besides, of course, her younger brother, Tad, who had Down syndrome and gave Benjamin the creeps. Tad ran up to him when he first got there, and said, "A star!" and placed a gold-star sticker on his arm. Benjamin ignored him and went to change in the men's locker room. When he came back out in his orange swim trunks, Lucy said, "You're too skinny. I can count your ribs," in such a way that let him know she approved.

Nestled on a hill, the Briarwood Country Club had a great view of the town, which blinked in the distance like a steely mirage. The sky was bleached white, and the adults had left the pool area for the inside. Benjamin was the first to enter the pool, cannonballing into the water. The girls plopped in right after, and soon the air was thick with the smell of chlorine. Lucy was the last to get in the water, easing in one leg at a time. As she started to paddle his way, Benjamin cupped his hands and dipped them just below the surface of the pool. Then he started pelting her with cold blasts of water. "It's better," he explained, "if you get wet all at once."

"Bastard," she said, but her lips were crooked in a half smile, telling Benjamin that she thought he was flirting. He wasn't. Besides always being a little aggravated with her, he didn't find her especially attractive. Her face was long, like a mule's, and her belly was squishy and poked out, a marshmallow that she hid even now by wearing a T-shirt over her bathing suit.

Lucy suggested that they play Marco Polo and picked Benjamin as "it." Suddenly, the other girls splashed away in all directions. The squeals were so sharp that Benjamin felt his teeth chatter. He didn't want to play but figured that after he tagged someone he'd suggest a new game, perhaps chicken fighting. He closed his eyes and waited for the movements to quiet. "Marco," he called, which was followed by a few shrill shouts and then a choir of voices giddily sounding from every direction. "Polo," they shouted. He swam quickly to his right, thinking the weaker among them had migrated to the shallow end. "Marco," he called again, sloshing in the water, swinging his arms, hoping to touch a stray arm, the edge of a shoulder, and end the game once and for all. But this time, there was no response. The water had grown still, silent, almost as if he were now the only one in the pool. "Marco," he called again. "Marco, Marco." It was spooky. He began to think that they were playing some kind of joke on him. He pounded his fists in the water. "What the fuck," he said finally, opening his eyes. The girls were all clutching the various sides of the pool, their heads turned away from him, looking the other direction. Nearest to him was Lucy. She paddled over, and whispered, "Daddy has this place reserved. They shouldn't be here." Benjamin only half heard her. He, like the others in the water, was captivated by the strange figure standing at the edge of the pool, a girl with two heads.

IT ALL MADE SENSE to him now, the affliction his aunt had been talking about. The Cade twins were conjoined twins, fused at the shoulder, sharing the same body from the clavicle down. Or maybe they were two half bodies smashed into one; Benjamin wasn't sure. His mind began flashing as soon as he saw them, trying to think of ways to comprehend their existence: They were different knuckles on the same finger; each a separate tip on a snake's forked tongue. Two, but one. One, but two.

They wore a large terry-cloth bathrobe and a pair of bright yellow slippers. Their blond hair was identical in shade but done in different fashions. The girl on the left, the one with softer eyes and thinner lips, had hers tied behind her head in a tight braid while the other one—her face all angles: high cheekbones, a sharp chin—let her hair fall freely about her shoulders in thick cascading waves. They looked about sixteen, and when they threw back the robe, they revealed a pair of toned legs and two elegant arms. The one-piece they wore looked as if it had been made especially for them, fitting over their long shoulders and around their slightly disproportionate breasts, giving their body a smooth finish. Benjamin inspected them as if they were some object Mr. Tuttleworth had displayed for him to sketch and noticed that their fingernails had French tips, just like those of a debutante.

"Jesus," he said, blinking. "Jesus Christ on a cross."

"Ridiculous," Lucy was saying, and when the twins sidled onto the diving board, the girls started pulling themselves out of the water. The twins didn't seem to take notice of their scattering, their eyes were fixed straight ahead at something above the other girls' heads. By the time they had made it to the end of the board, the pool held only Benjamin, who could not be moved. Everyone seemed to be watching them; some of the adults had even ventured back outside. The twin on the right smirked, appearing to revel in being the center of attention, and the other one was mumbling something, her eyes hard and focused. They extended their arms and, in one fluid motion, dove into the water, causing barely a splash. The adults applauded, but the twins didn't resurface right away to hear them. Instead, they swam under the water, making their way slowly to Benjamin's end of the pool.

Meanwhile, a woman wearing a pink straw hat and a long multicolored caftan ambled outside. "My nieces," she was saying to some of the adults. "They out here?" The twins resurfaced a few feet in front of Benjamin, their eyes clear and blue and completely startling. They turned their heads in unison and watched the woman in the caftan approach.

"Told you she wouldn't be happy," said the one with the braid.

"What a killjoy," said the other. "I'm not spending all summer cloistered in that house like a nun."

The woman traipsed to the edge of the pool and leaned down. "Girls," she said. "Thought I said to stay in the game room." She removed her sunglasses, glanced at Benjamin, then back at the twins. "What are you wearing?"

"Made it ourselves with Mama."

"Isn't it lovely? Fits us like a dream." The one on the right was grinning. She was trouble, Benjamin could sense it. Up close, he saw that her face was so perfect in its dimensions that he wanted to reach out and touch her cheeks. He waded closer to them, ignoring Lucy who was calling him, telling him it was time to cut the cake. The twins snapped their heads back to him when he neared them. They gazed at him as if he were the strangest thing they'd ever seen.

"Yes?" said the one on the right.

"I'm an artist," he said, and they chuckled.

The aunt stood and put her sunglasses back on. "It's time to go."

"Who are you?" said the one on the left.

He told them his name, and the one on the right raised an eyebrow. "You're that preacher's kid," she said. "Oh, we've heard all about you."

"You're bad," the one on the left said. They laughed again, this time much louder.

Benjamin pressed on. He knew what he wanted now. He said, "I'm an artist, and I'd like to draw you."

The twins went silent, and the one on the right was about to say something, but the aunt was clapping her hands now, as if that might get them out of the pool faster. "Out, out," she said to them. They fell back into the water and backstroked to the diving board, then they climbed out using the metal ladder and put on their bathrobe, leaving the question he'd asked unanswered and floating in the air like a forgotten balloon.

AUNT BEATRICE MET BENJAMIN at his bedroom door that morning, and said, "Your father is having one of his spells." This meant that his father had become obsessed with something and had decided to see it through. A month ago, he had decided to uproot the flower garden in the back—the garden Benjamin's mother had planted when they'd moved there—and cover it with pine-smelling wood chips. The first Sunday Aunt Beatrice was staying with them, he snaked the drains, causing the half bathroom in the hall to flood. Benjamin had found her ankle-deep in the water, on the verge of tears. "He ain't crazy," he said to her. "Just sad."

That morning his father was in the living room. The windows had been stripped of their curtains and blinds, which lay in a pile on the love seat. His father nodded at him, and said, "Have to fix these. Hang them right. The sun keeps getting in."

"Okay, Daddy." Benjamin helped his father hook the blinds back to the windows, then handed him the curtains.

When they finished, his father stepped back away from the windows, sighed, and said, "Well, I guess that is as good as it's going to get." He left for the kitchen, and Benjamin followed.

His aunt was frying thin slices of salt meat in a large black skillet, and she smiled at them when they came walking in. Her hair was twisted in curlers, and she was nursing a cup of coffee. "All situated," she said, speaking to Benjamin, who nodded.

The kitchen, like the rest of the parsonage, was small and barely had room for the three of them, but Benjamin knew better than to complain: The Second Baptist Church had allowed them to rent the place even though his father no longer preached there—the official statement was that he was "on leave." Aunt Beatrice set a plate in front of him, and said, "Heard you saw those Cade girls at Briarwood the other day. You know their mother sends them to some artsy-fartsy school up north. That's why they're so bold."

"They are good divers." He grabbed the bottle of syrup and poured it on the meat. With a fork, he squished the meat around in the gooeyness before eating it. He enjoyed the salty-sweet combination. His father picked at his food, nibbling the edges of some toast before giving up altogether and hiding behind the large gray wall of a newspaper.

"They should be more careful." Aunt Beatrice took his father's plate and slid it into the sink behind her. "So sad. Those girls haven't got a chance."

"Not many of us seem to," Benjamin said, his mouth full of mush. He swallowed. "But I don't think they're sad at all."

"I just mean," Aunt Beatrice said, her voice rising an octave at being challenged, "it must be a burden to them to live in such a way. Can only imagine what that mother was thinking leaving them here while she up and—"

His father coughed and folded the paper as neatly as he'd found it. "I think," he said, "we should get a move on. We'll be late." His voice was deep and piercing. Aunt Beatrice seemed taken aback by the suddenness of his voice and downed her coffee as if there were something stronger than caffeine in it. Benjamin, on the other hand, missed his father's voice, the richness and unadorned confidence of it. Missed listening to it each Sunday.

The Second Baptist Church was on Miller Avenue and shared a parking lot with the Jitney Jungle across the street. The church was built in the late '80s and didn't have a steeple or a baptismal. It was a squat, beige-bricked building with darkly colored stained-glass windows and a long sidewalk that snaked around a memory garden, which had a rosebush planted in his mother's honor. They were so late that they didn't tarry through the fellowship hall, but went straight to the front door, which had already been closed. His father had been the founding preacher here, and Benjamin felt nervousness and some other type of emotion he couldn't place prickle off his father when they entered the building. The last two pews were empty, as always, and he followed his aunt and father into the very last one. Very few people turned to regard them as they took their seats since the choir was performing the offertory hymn. The sound of the organ and the piano drowned out the singing voices; Benjamin imagined the noise as one large eraser pushing against their throats.

After they finished singing, the new preacher strode to the pulpit. Brother Tim had been the youth director back in the days of Benjamin's father. Benjamin didn't trust him: He seemed too relaxed and feigned coolness—wearing a shiny pair of New Balances and a Ralph Lauren polo to preach in—as if he'd invented how to be cool, as if he and God had nicknames for each other. His father treated God as if He were a wizened professor; this guy treated God as if He were a frat brother. And it also didn't help matters that every time he spotted Benjamin, Brother Tim always regaled him with the same old joke: "Hey, Benjamin, how you *ben jammin'*? I've ben jammin' with JC! Ha, ha, ha!"

Brother Tim welcomed the congregation and then led them in a prayer. Then he smiled and did one of his "cool" laughs that made Benjamin squirm. "Today," he said, "we have such a treat for you. A visiting duo has asked to come sing for us, and let me tell you"—Brother Tim put his hand sideways against his lips as if he were telling the congregation a secret—"these little ladies can sure sing: Beth and Bella Cade."

The Cade sisters, who had been sitting in the front row, stood up and walked to the center of the aisle in front of the pulpit. They were dressed conservatively, wearing a knee-length plaid skirt and a square gray jacket that hugged their shoulders, making them seem narrower than they were. Their blond hair was identical: each had a tight bun behind the head.

"Lord be my helper," Aunt Beatrice whispered. There was a long silence in the church as the congregation appraised them and the girls situated themselves to be appraised. As they had done when they were on the diving board, they gazed out above the pews at some imagined object. They clasped hands, and the one on the left spoke first.

"We will be singing 'Beulah Land.'" She nodded to her sister, then they started singing, and it felt to Benjamin as if someone had turned on a CD player. Their voices, their harmonies, were that perfect to his ear. Listening to them, he thought about what his aunt had said about them earlier that morning, about it being a burden to be them: physically attached to another for the remainder of your life. But it occurred to him that it wasn't a burden at all, that it was, in fact, a gift to have someone always there at your shoulder who knew you as well as—or better than—you knew yourself.

The girls' voices rose and rose, to the exposed rafters, filling up every crevice of the church, leaking out the windows. Somewhere, midway through the performance, his collar began to bother him. His throat was itchy, and the voices, though beautiful, were somehow making it worse. He longed for them to finish, but the song seemed to go on and on. He sat on his hands and resisted the urge to scream. In front of him, he noticed the empty pew was shaking. He freed one of his hands and touched it, the vibrating causing him to shake as well, as if an electric current passed through him. He glanced at his aunt, who clutched his father's knee, and whispered to Benjamin, "Maybe he'll stop when they finish." Beside her sat his father, hunched over, gripping the pew ahead of him, trembling violently.

MR. TUTTLEWORTH'S HOUSE was an old Queen Anne Victorian located on Tollivar Street in the historic district of town near the square. In addition to being painted a bright pink, the house had a three-story tower on the east end where Benjamin imagined the old artist sat for hours upon hours working on his latest canvas. Benjamin and Lucy were his only students who kept up with the lessons during the summer. They met in his large study that was cluttered with African masks and brightly colored vignettes from Spain and South America. In the corner, where Mr. Tuttleworth sometimes sat while they were drawing, were a knight's armor and a spinning wheel that still retained an actual spindle. While Benjamin sat behind his sketch pad, he often wondered how easy it would be to get lost in Mr. Tuttleworth's house. Get lost and never be heard from again: The thought was appealing.

Today the teacher was droning on about the importance of shading, of the hard line, the particular stroke, and Benjamin, still reeling from the twins' Sunday performance, heard very little. Also, he was ready to move beyond the simple objects his teacher put before him to draw. The chalky apples, the fluted melons, always paired with some strange artifact Mr. Tuttleworth had unearthed from the clutter of his house—it was boring, so lifeless, when compared to what he'd seen at the country club and the church.

At one point during the lecture, Benjamin raised his hand. "Mr. Tuttleworth," he said. "When are we going to draw other stuff?"

Mr. Tuttleworth clicked his tongue, considering the question. "Other stuff?" Lucy gawked at Benjamin; normally, she was the one who spoke in class.

"Yeah," Benjamin continued. "Like people. You know, real things."

"Ah," the teacher muttered. "People. You're not ready." He proceeded to tell Benjamin that he hadn't found his voice as an artist yet and probably wouldn't for some time, that he needed to spend his youth focusing on technique. Let the "challenging pieces" come in their due moment. After all, he'd been drawing for only a little more than a year.

"My voice?"

"Yes. Your voice. Perhaps better to say your eye: the part of your imagination that is different and unique from everyone else's. One of the biggest challenges is discovering what you see about the world that no one else does, and then you have to execute it brilliantly."

Lucy's hand shot in the air, but she spoke before she was called on. "What if," she asked, "you can't find it—this eye-voice thingy. What if everything's already been taken and how you see the world is just a copy of somebody else's?"

Mr. Tuttleworth adjusted the black-rimmed glasses on his nose, pushing them closer to his eyes. He had a lumpy figure and wore his pants too high to be comfortable. "Well, then," he said, and put his hands in his pockets. "I think if that is the case, truly the case, then you've just figured out whether or not you are really an artist."

After class, Lucy asked Benjamin if he wanted to come to her house for a snack. Her father was a well-to-do ophthalmologist, and her family lived just outside of town in a small suburb filled with rows and rows of brick houses, the kind of houses with neat lawns and polished shutters that Benjamin saw on TV shows when the family was supposed to be upper middle class, though, in truth, in the Delta, living in such houses meant you were basically rich. The walk to her house seemed to him to be one of the longest in his life. They moved at a sluggish pace—Lucy not being a fast walker—down Hutchinson Street, which crossed the railroad tracks, passed the old grain elevator, and led straight to her family's little cul-de-sac. Lucy kept talking about this book she was reading—some exaggerated romance with lizard people and vampire-werewolf hybrids—and by the time they reached her house, he was ready to turn around and go back home. But then he remembered that Lucy lived near where the twins were living with their aunt. He asked her which one of the houses was the twins', and she said, "Oh, them. They're one street over." She pointed in the direction of the house. "Their house is the only two-story on their street."

"I don't think I've ever met someone like them before."

"Ha," Lucy said, sniffing. "I've seen the likes before. The way they talk! Like some kind of Ole Miss bitch."

Benjamin sighed. In that moment, he decided that he could never like Lucy. After leaning his bike against the mailbox, he followed her inside the house, wanting a glass of water, then he'd make up some excuse to leave. The rooms were quiet, and she explained to him that her mother had taken her brother to the movies. They sat on uncomfortable barstools in the kitchen area and drank tall glasses of orange juice and ate two Fruit Roll-Ups apiece. Benjamin was licking his sticky fingers when she asked, "So what made you speak up in class today about drawing people?"

Benjamin thought for a minute. He didn't want to tell her his plan for the Cade twins because he knew she'd be against the whole thing. She was probably, after all, still smarting from their stealing some of the attention at her birthday party. So he said that he was just curious, just tired of the same old shit.

She nodded, and then her eyes got wide with an idea. "Let's go listen to some of my CDs in my room," she said, and grabbed his hand. Her touch was clammy and rough, and he snatched his hand out of her grasp, which she didn't seem to notice.

"May need to start heading back," he said, jumping off the barstool. He realized that this was the first time he'd ever been alone with a girl, at her house, with no parents nearby. And she had just asked him to her bedroom. His lips felt dry and coarse against his gums when he smiled and said that he needed to go.

"One song. My sound system is top-notch. Got it for Christmas last year."

She skipped back to her room, her fingers trailing along the walls. Benjamin eyed his bicycle from the living-room window. He could make a run for it if he wanted. *Fucking man up*, he told himself. *She's just a girl. A fat girl.*

Her room was swathed in various posters of country music singers. Tracy Lawrence was tacked on the wall above her headboard while Patty Loveless and Suzy Bog-guss shared a space on her closet door. The room made him uncomfortable, all those eyes watching him. He sat on the floor and crossed his legs, which appeared to disappoint Lucy who sat on the bed. She flopped back on the mattress with an exaggerated fall. For the next ten minutes, they listened to two tracks from Bonnie Raitt's album *Street-lights*. After the second song ended, he stood and said that it was getting late. This was the truth: The sun was bleed-ing red light through her room's window.

"Wait," she said, and circled her fingers around his wrist. "Listen to one more. The next track is 'Angel from Montgomery.' It's the one I wanted you to hear in the first place." He nodded, and she turned on the song. When it began to play, she moved closer to him, eyes shut, mouth wet and open. He ducked from her kiss and stepped back to the door.

"Really," he said. "I got shit to do."

The hurt on her face was evident, almost made her somewhat beautiful for a moment. His stomach felt queasy as he stumbled down the hall, and when he was outside in the fresh air, he began to feel more at ease with himself. He hopped on his bike and pedaled across the street and then turned and backtracked, cycling his way up the next street over. It didn't take him long to find the only two-story house on that road. He left his bike a few houses down and snuck through the backyards. Evening was coming on heavy, and there wasn't much light left when he made it to the yard. The house had pale vinyl siding and thick storm windows; the second floor looked just as roomy as the first. Three tall windows looked down the street from the second floor, and he tried to imagine which one was the twins' bedroom. Large shrubs outlined the house; they were dry and scrubby from the summer heat. He went up to them and waved his hands over the prickly sprigs, feeling them break and crumble under the pads of his fingers. From above, he heard a sound—a heavy footstep or a door closing. He looked up just in time to see the white curtains being drawn.

LATER THAT NIGHT, he was in his room doodling in his notebook. He did all his practice drawings in the cheap notebooks his aunt bought him at the grocery store. The blue horizontal lines took the pressure off his own lines being perfect. He was trying to draw the twins' faces, but they hadn't come out right: he wasn't able to capture that sense of awe he'd experienced at the pool. Instead, their faces, linked to the same shoulder, kept looking more and more like a caricature. His window was open, and the balmy night air blew into his room, smelling of fruity detergent. His aunt was washing clothes in the carport next to his room, and the dull racket of the washing machine filled the house. Then the phone rang. After two rings, someone picked up.

He looked up from his notebook and found his aunt standing in the doorway, looking down at him. "Phone for you," she said. "Some girl." There was a slight mocking smile on her face. Benjamin couldn't help himself; he blushed. He figured it was probably Lucy.

"Benjamin," the voice said when he placed the receiver to his ear, and he knew immediately who it was. "This is Bella Cade. We met at the country club."

He almost dropped the phone. "Yes, Bella. Good. Fine." The tone of her voice was confident and direct, same as it was that day in the pool. He felt his back tighten as they continued to talk. He experienced the sensation of falling, as if he were hurtling down the long dip on a roller coaster.

"We were thinking about your offer for us to be your— What was that word again, sister? Oh, yes, your offer for us to be your objets d'art."

HE MET THEM two days later when he decided to skip art class and go straight to their house. The twins greeted him at the back door wearing a pair of skinny jeans and an oversize purple T-shirt. Their hair was damp and wavy, and smelled like strawberry soap. "You're late," Bella said. They moved out of the way to let him enter. The inside of the house looked vaguely like the inside of Lucy's house; the interior had this glossy sheen the parsonage lacked. Benjamin wondered what a woman without any kids did with so much space. When the twins shut the door behind him, the falling sensation came back to him, that slow tug downward into darkness.

"We don't have a lot of time today," Beth said. "Aunt Viv doesn't stay long at the beauty shop."

"Not as long as she should," Bella interjected. She nodded for him to follow them. They walked upstairs to their room, which had only a bed and a behemoth chest of drawers that took up most of a whole wall. The natural light in the room made everything shimmer. Benjamin studied how easily they walked, each one—he assumed—controlling the function of one of the legs. Their coordination was excellent. They sat on the bed and stared at him, their eyes an unreal ocean blue, and he realized that they were expecting him to speak.

"So," he said, and showed them his satchel. "I brought my sketch pad. I guess we can do it here. The light's about perfect."

"On the contrary," Bella said. "We want to see your work first. Make sure we aren't, you know, wasting our time."

This peeved Benjamin. "Work?"

"Yes," said Beth, her voice much quieter and more reasonable sounding than Bella's. "How do we know if you are any good or not?"

He laughed, thinking at first that they must be teasing him, but neither face so much as suggested a smile. He shuffled through the stuff in his bag and pulled out his sketch pad. "I only have what I've been doing for class. Nothing special."

"That'll do."

He flipped to one of his cleanest drawings, the one he had slaved over for more than a month: a row of books bookended on either side by a tomato. He was best at circles, which made him figure he could render a face fairly easily. He gave them the pad. They gazed at the drawing for what seemed to Benjamin like the entire afternoon. While they were appraising his work, Bella fumbled with the little nightstand by the bed, pulling out a pack of Virginia Slims and a neon-green lighter.

"Sister?" she said, and Beth set the drawings aside and lit her sister's cigarette. Bella took a long drag and then threw back her head and exhaled smoke.

"Open the window," Beth said. "Aunt Viv'll have our hide."

Benjamin motioned for them to keep their seats and went to open it for them.

"A gentleman," Beth said.

"Not anything like we heard. Picking fights, causing trouble." Bella took another long drag, seemingly to savor the taste of it. "Seriously, though, this artwork is shit."

"I can do better," he said quickly. "I just need the right subject. The right motivation."

"I'll admit that there's a rawness here I like very much," Beth said.

"You're too nice," Bella said.

"Oh, give him a break."

Bella lifted her hand. "All right, all right. Some of

this"—she was flipping through the pages again as she spoke—"is passable. But the boy is no Cézanne."

"Do we really want a Cézanne?"

"No, but I don't want our portrait to look like a Picasso either. Tell me, sister, do you want your ears attached somewhere below your waist? Aren't we unique enough?"

Beth turned toward Benjamin, who'd been watching the interaction between the two faces, silent and fascinated. Fascinated, that is, by the ease with which they communicated with each other but also terrified and—if he were honest with himself—a little angered by how dismissive they were of his work. "So we will be your first," Beth said, and Bella, dumping her ashes into the open drawer, giggled. They stopped talking and seemed to be pondering something. Benjamin knew they shared skin and blood, but he wondered if they could share thoughts too.

"Okay," Bella said, finally. "We will let you draw us. But we want a copy of it when you finish— No, the original."

"For our mother," Beth said. "She'll like it."

Benjamin was nodding as they spoke. They set up dates and times for them to meet for the rest of the summer before they headed back home to Kentucky in mid-August.

Before he left, he had to ask, "Why me? Why are you doing this?"

Bella smiled, showing her white teeth. "Because," she said, "when you look at us, we feel powerful." She closed her eyes and took a final puff of her cigarette. "We feel—I feel—like a god."

BENJAMIN STOPPED GOING to Mr. Tuttleworth's altogether and pedaled over twice a week to visit the Cade sisters and work on his sketches of them. He started small with his new project, examining their faces closely at first. Really, he soon learned, the human face was simple enough in its architecture: a series of footballs—eyes, nose holes, lips. Ovals that were pinched at the ends. He made them sit in the bay window in the living room, where the light caught the gold in their hair and made them almost glow. By the middle of July, he had filled up two sketch pads' worth of "practices." He had pages devoted to their eyes and their noses (Beth's was smoother than Bella's) and their chins (he could draw their faces with his eyes closed now and thought he might never forget them, that they would stay with him always), but very few of his sketches focused on them below the neck. That part of them intimidated him. Each time he tried, the figure came out sloppy and ill made, with Beth shaking her head at it and Bella saying he wasn't "seeing them right."

One day the twins were going through his latest attempts at their body, flipping through the pages and Bella smacking her lips. "Something is still not right. You seem to be holding back. Sister?" Bella said. "Is this really how our body looks?"

Beth sighed. "This is a fine torso, but it is not our torso. Not nearly as complex or multidimensional as it needs to be. Think we are asking too much of him?"

Benjamin coughed. "Uh, I'm still here." He shifted in his seat in front of them. They had a way of making him feel like he was the one on display, not them, and he didn't like it. Ultimately, he was doing the drawing for himself, and so far, he was happy with his progress. They, obviously, were not, and he was coming to understand that maybe they never would be.

"Just not good enough," Bella was saying. "Come here."

Bella patted the cushion on her side of the seat, so he sat there.

"Listen," she said, taking his hand and placing it against her chest. "This here is my heartbeat. Feel it?" He nodded, and Beth took his other hand and brought it to her side of their chest.

"And this one," she said, "is mine." They dropped their hands, but he kept his palms pressed against them. He felt the tiny undulations of their hearts, pumping fresh blood to all of their organs. "Understand us. You have to understand us if you want to make what you are doing worth a damn."

"See how my heartbeat is just a bit stronger than hers,"

Bella said, and Benjamin closed his eyes. Yes, he soon could feel the difference: Her heart thumped just a little more forcefully than her sister's. "I'm what the doctors call the dominant one. There's more of me here than there is of her."

"I'll give out sooner," Beth said, and leaned her head against her sister's.

"But I won't be far behind. What? Two minutes tops."

Benjamin removed his hands. "Are you scared?" he asked Beth. "Of giving out faster, I mean. Being the first to go."

"Oh, no," she said. "I'm the lucky one. Won't have to know what it is like without this one here nagging me."

"Benjamin," Bella said. "We want to understand you too."

"Yes," Beth said. "Please."

They asked him to tell them about his mother. He knew that this was a way of bonding themselves to one another, revealing their vulnerabilities. He didn't mind because, although they were not the first who had asked him to talk about his mother, they were the first who seemed genuinely interested in what he had to say about her.

"She was a painter," he said. "Did that mural in the fellowship hall of Second Baptist of all those Old Testament characters." After his mother's funeral, the repast was held in that room, and he remembered not being able to take his eyes off of those figures on the wall—Abraham, Moses, David, Esther, Ruth—that his mother had created, thinking how strange it was that they seemed to persist even though she did not. He tried to explain this to the twins, but he felt it somehow got all mangled and confused.

The twins were staring intently at him when he finished. "Tell me," Bella said. "Have you ever kissed a girl?"

He shook his head, and they leaned forward.

That night he dreamed about the twins, about how he'd kissed both of them: first Bella, who'd nipped at his lips with her teeth, and then Beth, who'd allowed him to press into her, steal her breath. He dreamed that he was between them, conjoined to their body. He wasn't much more than a head atop their shoulders. "You'll have to share our hearts," Beth said matter-of-factly. "It's the only way."

THE NEXT WEEK the twins had an idea for how to improve his work on their torso. "Nude," Bella told him. "Our body, for better or worse, in the raw. So you can get a better look." Benjamin was drinking Dr Pepper at the time and almost spit it out of his mouth when he fully understood what they were proposing. He could tell by the way Beth wouldn't meet his eyes that it was mainly Bella's idea.

"I don't know," he said.

Bella smiled. "It'll make the drawing sing." She told him that they had talked over the pros and cons, and were both willing to do this. The world became very small to

Benjamin as he listened to her talk; it seemed to shrink and become just them. He didn't know what to do with his hands and looked for his pencils in his satchel. While they went to the bathroom to change, Benjamin closed the blinds, and when they returned, the living room was dark and quiet. Benjamin was sitting on the coffee table, not knowing where to look. They were wearing the same terry-cloth robe that they'd worn at the pool party, which now seemed long ago. Beth's hand clutched the robe close to their chest, her trembling as evident as Benjamin's. Only Bella appeared to be calm. "It's okay," she said, and he wasn't sure if she was speaking to him or her sister. "This is something the Lord hath made," she added, her voice sounding more serious than he'd ever heard it. She grasped her sister's hand and moved it down to her waist. She unclasped the belt of the robe, and it fell to their ankles.

They moved to the couch, but Benjamin stopped them. "No," he said. "Keep standing. Please."

Bella smiled and nodded, and Beth looked above his head and appeared to be mumbling something. Benjamin, unable to swallow, taking in what was before him, went to work tracing the strange geography of their skin. Their breasts were different and beautiful in their own way: Bella's hung heavy and round, her nipple a stubby knot of pink, while Beth's was a pert scooping of flesh a bit smaller and more sensitive looking than Bella's. If he had to guess, Benjamin would assume that Bella had developed faster—but was that possible? He didn't know, and looking at them and feeling his penis go hard and press uncomfortably against his pants, he understood how little he knew about anything. Their figure got only more interesting the farther down his eyes went. They shared a rather large and startling belly button, which he knew many would find repulsive, but the sight of it only made him feel closer to them. As he was tracing the area between their legs, where a soft spray of yellow hair, curly and unkempt, disappeared between their closed thighs, he thought of Mr. Tuttleworth, of what the old teacher might say to him for drawing these girls. *I'll show you who's ready*, he imagined telling the man and tried to picture his teacher's face when he showed him the figure he was creating now on his pad.

Afterward, the twins looked over the piece, and Bella said, "Still looks like a cave drawing, but it's better." They were wearing the robe again, but it hung loose, untied.

He was standing close to them, peering over their shoulder, and could smell their eucalyptus body lotion and a darker scent underneath that. As if he were huffing spray paint, smelling them made him heady, dizzy even. He reached over and touched a patch of exposed flesh just below their belly button. The skin was soft, pliable. The room darkened. It was late in the afternoon, and he would have to leave them soon. The girls gazed down at his hand. "That's us, both of us," Beth said, and he moved his hand lower, hooking a finger inside them. "That too," said Bella, her voice catching. They stood there, the three of them, rocking, until Bella murmured, "No," and touched his wrist. When he took his hand away, his finger was slick with them—*their essence*, he thought, as he put the finger in his mouth.

BENJAMIN LEFT THEIR HOUSE immensely proud of his portrait and feeling as if his joints were made of air. A part of him wanted to take the portrait to Mr. Tuttleworth right away, but it didn't seem ready yet. As he was walking his bike out of the twins' driveway, someone stepped in front of him to block his path. Lucy.

"I've been watching you," she said. "Ever since you quit art class. I don't know exactly what you've been doing with them, but it's sick, whatever it is."

He felt as if he'd never seen Lucy until that moment. "Listen," he said. "I don't know what you—"

"Freaks," she blurted out. "And, what, they're your own personal carnival sideshow?"

"It's really none of your business." Benjamin was trying hard to remain calm; he wanted to hit Lucy in the throat, make it so she would never talk again.

"You are such a piece of shit, you know that?"

"All this just because I wouldn't suck your ugly face. Fuck you."

"You can't talk to me that way."

"Fatty," he said, the anger pulsating through him now, strong and steady. It'd been a long time since he'd exploded on someone, and he had forgotten how nice the release felt. "Moo!" he bellowed. "Moo!"

She stood there shaking, her hands tightly knuckled into fists.

Benjamin told her to get out of his way and shoved past her. Her next move surprised him: She rushed him, pushing him to the ground, his head slapping against the pavement. "Fuck me," he said. The papers in his satchel scattered across the blacktop. When he got himself back to his feet, Lucy was gone. It took him nearly half an hour to get his papers back into his satchel. He pushed his bike home, dazed. It was only later, when he was in his room, that he sensed—without even checking—that Lucy had stolen his nude picture of the twins.

HE BICYCLED TO LUCY'S HOUSE the next morning, not caring if her parents were home. What he found in the neighborhood shocked him. Taped on the light poles and sticking out of every mailbox were bright neon flyers, all fluorescent shades of pink and green. Some people were already outside taking them down, and when he snatched one that had blown into the street and saw what was on it, he almost threw up. There was his drawing of the twins, their nude figure, their immediate faces, only it had been rendered to look more exaggerated than he'd intended. The angles of their hips, the curve of their breasts—they had a mean, hard look to them that made his stomach suck in on itself as if a fist had just walloped him. Under the drawing were the words NEIGHBORHOOD WATCH: BEWARE THE GIRL WITH TWO HEADS!

He dropped his bike and raced down the street toward Lucy's house. The sun had not yet burned the morning mist away, and the house seemed to appear out of the clouds. He knocked on the front door, but there was no answer. The garage was empty, and he began to think that no one was home, but he heard a dull thump coming from the backyard. Tad, Lucy's brother, was jumping on a trampoline and waved at Benjamin when he saw him round the corner of the house. "Your sister," he told the boy, "is a cunt."

With that, he leaped onto the trampoline and tackled Tad. "A star! A star!" the boy was screaming as Benjamin pounded into him, feeling his knuckles tear against the boy's face. Then, something whizzed past his face; he felt something bite his shoulder. It was like a wasp sting only stronger, deeper. Behind him, Lucy stood on the deck, a BB gun leveled directly at him.

"Next one goes in your eye," she said. Her own eyes were red and swollen, and she looked like she hadn't slept in a week.

"How could you?" he said, getting off the boy, who was holding his face and muttering something.

"Leave." She motioned with her gun. "You're no good to anybody."

Benjamin jumped off the trampoline and walked out of the yard back to his bike. He didn't look back, though he swore he could hear Lucy Gatesmith crying. Told himself that she'd probably cry and cry long after he was gone.

THE NEWS OF WHAT HAPPENED—the flyers, which everyone assumed were all Benjamin's doing, and the assault of the Gatesmith boy—spread around town as fast as Benjamin figured it would. "Can't protect you this time," Aunt Beatrice said, meeting him at the door. "Vivian Cade called. Said she's a good mind to call the police. Said those girls are just distraught."

He didn't feel like talking or explaining himself. Let people think what they would; the only people he cared about were the girls. He knew that he would have to make it up to them.

"Where are you going?" his aunt said; he was halfway down the hall to his room. "Your father wants a word with you."

He hadn't been in his father's office since before his mother died. It was just as he remembered: books scattered everywhere, the thick smell of dust, the desk grainy and chipped. His father was standing by the tiny window that looked out into the street and holding one of the flyers. "You did this?" he said to Benjamin, and he shook the picture at him.

"Sort of. I was only—"

His father held up his hand. His hair was thinning and his face was creased in deep wrinkles. He'd never looked so old. "You drew these girls," he said, speaking as if he were trying to understand. "You drew them—naked."

"Yes, sir."

After studying the picture for some time, he began to laugh. His laughter was hoarse and heavy, and was as painful for Benjamin to hear as if he'd been slapped.

BENJAMIN SLIPPED OUT of his bedroom window with such ease that he wondered why he'd never done it before.

The night sky was clear: the Big and Little Dippers coasted above his head as he hurried into the night. Trees shook in the wind, black figures against a black sky. He made sure to wear dark clothes; he didn't want to be seen as he spirited through the town, heading toward the Cade house. It was half past eleven when he skidded to a stop in front of their house. The house was dark, and when he stepped into the yard, the grass crunched under his feet. Every sound seemed to echo and multiply in the darkness. Earlier that day, he'd selected pebbles carefully from the driveway—small smooth ones that would scratch against the glass but not break it. He had a pocket full of them.

His first few shots at the twins' window were poorly aimed and cracked against the shutters and the awning. But he got better. A few scraped across the window, and soon the room came alive with light. He saw their dark silhouette against the window. He waved, and the figure disappeared. He pressed his ear to the house to see if he could hear them walking down the stairs, but he heard nothing. The sound of crickets swelled up around him and made him sick with longing. If he could just see them one more time, he could explain everything. He could make it all right. If they'd let him. There were footsteps, quick little ones that pranced down the stairs. The door clicked open, and Benjamin scrambled over to see them. He was speaking, blurting it all out in one mash of vowels, before he realized that it was only the aunt standing in the doorway.

"You," she said, "need to leave. I am two seconds from calling the police."

"Please," he said, but he couldn't finish. He was crying, snot and tears dribbling down his face. "Please," he said again, and reached for the woman. She screamed then and slammed the door shut. He threw his body against the wooden frame. "Please," he screamed into the door. He slid down and rolled onto the grass and wallowed there until he calmed down some, until he could think. In the distance, he thought he heard sirens. *Let them come*, he thought; he would be able to explain it to them. He would explain how he got there, on that front yard, to anyone who would listen. Once the words started rolling out of his mouth, they might never stop.

THE EXAGGERATIONS

I longed for the days when I was young enough to be switched with crape myrtle.

—LEWIS NORDAN,
"Sugar Among the Chickens"

SWEET AND LOW

I.

Forney's mother spends the whole morning cleaning their dusty farmhouse from top to bottom. Beginning with the dining room, she dusts the china cabinet and the upholstered chairs. Adds a leaf to the table, then drapes it with a freshly starched and pressed tablecloth embroidered with bright yellow flowers. She vacuums the carpet in the living room—the sudden blast of the Hoover waking Forney, his first indication that today will be an unusual one—and she sweeps the hardwood floor in the den, her broom finding every mote of dirt, every knotty cobweb. Finally, she varnishes the upright piano in the hallway, taking her time with the old Steinway, until it gleams. Before Forney comes downstairs, she moves the pewter urn containing his father's ashes from atop the piano to some other location. Out of sight. Perhaps to her bedroom.

All of this cleaning is a rare and sudden occurrence—Forney knows his mother loathes housework and hasn't touched a dishrag since his father's death the year before.

She barely glances his way when he comes into the kitchen, reporting casually over her shoulder that a man will be joining them for dinner tonight. His name's Buck Dickerson. "Oh, a friend," she says, when Forney asks who that is. She ignores his other questions—*Where did you meet him? Why is he coming?*—giving, instead, the full measure of her attention to the grout around the kitchen sink.

Her response does not alarm or even frustrate Forney. That is their way with each other: distant, with an air of suspicion. Whatever quality that's required to bind mother and son in affection lies dormant in them. He and his mother had once been united in their love for his father—the rawboned, benevolent, somewhat clumsy man he was. Perhaps if he had survived the heart attack, they could have kept on ignoring the hollowness between them. Kept on pretending, for his father's sake at least, that everything was all right. But in his absence, they have become more and more like strangers. The gap, Forney suddenly realizes as he leaves her in the kitchen, is too wide to cross.

According to the TV, a summer storm is headed their way, and by noon, thunder's echoing off the river bottom. In the kitchen, New York strips thaw in the sink and half a bag of Russet potatoes soak in a large silver pot in the refrigerator.

Restless, Forney opens the front door and gazes at the bruised sky and the pockets of light slicing through it. He sprawls out in the breezeway, pressing his bare feet against the loose mesh of the screen door. For a while, he reads *A Separate Peace*, then dozes, the smell of freshly tilled silt and raw pesticide wafting inside every now and then, tingling his nose. The farmhouse is cornered on all sides by fields and forest. They are what people in the Delta refer to as "rural," a term his mother despises.

He can hear her behind him. Bustling about the house. His mother is a tall woman with robust shoulders. She keeps her waves of blond hair sprayed into a great fortress above her head. At times, Forney even admires the heft of it, how it seems to defy gravity. He freely admits that she is pretty. In her own way. And he suspects that eleven years ago she was a knockout. His father, Reuben Culpepper, probably didn't have much of a chance against her looks. Supposedly, as the story goes, he first saw her at a nightclub in Dallas, the lead singer for an all-female group called the Silver-Ringed Gypsies, a Stevie Nicks cover band. "Heard her sing 'Gold Dust Woman,'" he told Forney. "That's all it took."

One thing he knows for sure about his mother: She did

love his father. Almost as much as Forney did. Overwhelming evidence supports this. She did, after all, leave Texas and move with him to Mississippi, which she calls, on a regular basis, the Absolute Center of Nowhere. And she abandoned her so-called promising music career. To top it off, she even bore him a son and gave motherhood an honest shake. Well, the best shake she *could* have given it. While there's not a single doubt in Forney's head that she eventually regretted each of these decisions, the impetus to make them must have been rooted in love, or something close to it.

When she finds him half-asleep on the floor, she shoos him back on up to his room. "I can't have you up under me, Forney. Not today."

Not ever, Forney wants to say as he stomps up the narrow staircase.

Back in his bedroom, he plops down on his mattress while outside his window the sky darkens. He eventually goes to his closet. And locates, in the back behind his khaki pants, his father's ratty old work jacket. A beige Carhartt. He puts the sleeves to his face and inhales the twang of hemp in the fabric, the scent of the lotion his father once wore on his hands to keep them from cracking during the wintertime. It's like a time machine, smelling the coat. One deep sniff, and *pow*: Dad's there again. After flicking off the light, he slides down to the floor, nuzzling the jacket shamelessly. There's a desire in him to crawl farther into the closet. Cocoon himself amid the safety of empty clothes.

Outside, rain slaps gently against the house. Lightning illumines the room—his messy bed, his poster of E.T. and Michael Jackson—and is followed by a clap of thunder.

Downstairs, the shower in his mother's bedroom cuts on. The sound of it sickens him. When the water warms up, she will disrobe and step in and clean herself. Get ready for Buck. Before today, it has never occurred to him that his mother would ever have a man over. A man who isn't his father.

Buck Dickerson—the name alone suggests that Forney will not like the man it belongs to. Probably one of those übermasculine types. Wide shouldered, protein guzzler. Loud, boisterous. Will call Forney "sport." Or worse: "son."

EVENING, and there's still the steady rain.

The smell of meat fills the house, eventually luring Forney back downstairs. Also: He's decided not to hide in his room like some scared child. No, sir. The house is just as much his as it is his mother's, so he has made it up in his mind to meet Mr. Buck Dickerson face-to-face when he comes traipsing in. Let him know how it is from the start.

His mother is slicing open baked potatoes and arranging them in a glass casserole dish when he trudges into the kitchen. She looks up at him and smiles, a new woman. She's wearing a demure navy skirt with a white blouse. Looking churchy. Almost Pentecostal. Gone is the fluffy hair, the heavy makeup. Now her hair's pulled back into an understated bun, revealing her delicate ears and a wrinkleless forehead.

"You like?" She models for him.

He grunts and asks her where all her hair went.

"Still here." She shakes her head, and the bun bounces stiffly. "Just better tamed."

"Dad liked it big."

She slams the last potato into the glass dish. "We are about new beginnings tonight."

"Is this a date?"

She laughs. Tells him that Buck is a special man. Going to be a big help to her. "Big help," she repeats, for emphasis.

"Help how?"

"He's got connections." She gives him this look that says: *You're too young to understand*. And the thing is, he doesn't understand. The whole day's been one bizarre turn after another. He tells her so too. At this, she rubs her temples—which, in her language, means *Look out!*—and says for him to stop worrying her, for Christ's sake.

So he goes into the living room. He sits on the couch and waits. Eyeing the door.

As the evening wears on, there's no sign of Buck. And

his mother returns her attention to the house. Frantically goes from room to room in her flats. Adjusting the distance between the chairs and the table. Arranging and then rearranging the place mats. Sweeping the rug in the breezeway. Her movements are jerky. *Like her body's running on electricity,* Forney thinks. Finally, she retreats to the front porch. Forney follows. She fascinates him the way he suspects a scientist is fascinated by an experiment unfolding in his laboratory. She leans her body over the porch railing and observes the falling rain. She extends her arm and touches it.

"Maybe he changed his mind," Forney says.

She doesn't respond.

They stand like this for some time, a few paces apart. Waiting.

Just before he's about to suggest they go on back inside and eat dinner before it gets cold, a pair of headlights blasts up the driveway. A horn honks. A Crown Victoria the color of a Sprite can bulldozes through the yard over an untended flower bed and parks beside the porch. A voice calls out from the darkness, begging to be forgiven for his lateness.

Forney moves beside his mother at the railing to get a better look. Preparing himself for the worst. First thing he notices about Buck is his height. He's not much taller than Forney is. Which is, for some reason, a relief to the boy. Once under the awning, he shrugs off his raincoat, and

Forney blurts out, "Holy moly." Buck's body looks like the reflection of a body in a fun-house mirror. All misshapen. Withered. His arms are painfully thin, not much more than skin and bone, and his legs appear too long for his crooked torso. He suffers—Forney will later learn—from severe scoliosis. Born with a curved spine that threw the rest of his body's construction out of whack.

"You two live out in the boonies," Buck says to both of them, adding that he got lost about two turns back. Under one of his arms, he's carrying a green bottle of malbec.

Forney's mother takes Buck's damp coat and leads him inside without comment. Forney trails behind, too stunned for words. This is who she brings home after a year of playing the widow? Of all the menfolk in the world, she has to pick what? A carnival freak is what. A sideshow attraction. Dad is probably rolling in his grave—but then Forney remembers that his father was cremated and can't roll.

In the fully lit living room, Buck sets the bottle of wine on top of the TV. "Oh, Felicia, the hair is *perfecto*." Then he grasps her left hand and kisses her knuckles.

The air in the room changes. Forney's mother stiffens, and Forney explodes with laughter. How can he not? All of it—the strange man, his mother's appearance—smacks of the absurd. When outdone, his father used to say, "I'm on a ship of fools, and it's sinking fast, brother!" Looking at these two, Forney almost recites it to them, but the look on his mother's face stalls him. She snatches her hand from Buck's as if it were scalded. "You stop that," she says, and it's unclear if she's reprimanding Forney or Buck or both of them. Her cheeks the color of a new radish, she turns away from them. Leaves them staring blankly at each other, wondering who was the one at fault, and plods off to the hall closet to put away Buck's raincoat.

OVER DINNER, Buck recounts with great relish how he first met Forney's mother. It was at, of all places, the Country Music Palace, the all-night karaoke bar near the interstate. The night he first noticed her, she was performing "Sleeping Single in a Double Bed," her clear-ringing voice completely bewitching him. Or so he claims. "Better than Mandrell," he tells Forney, who is enjoying the story and how Buck calls his mother "Bathsheba" when he refers to her in the narrative.

It's like Buck is speaking of another woman. Definitely not the mother Forney has known all these years, the stern-eyed woman who wears—except for tonight—shiny earrings and a mask of colorful makeup. He has had no idea that this singing is still so important to her. Isn't she too old? Almost thirty. And didn't she put that behind her when she decided to marry his father?

From across the table, he squints at her, trying to catch

a glimmer of this person Buck sees, this Bathsheba, big and tall, singing karaoke. Still, he can't picture it. No, not her. He doesn't know that woman at all. Doesn't want to either.

It also occurs to him, turning to study the man's face, that Buck Dickerson is almost handsome. There's a delicacy to his nose, the way it hooks above the lips. A richness to the olive-colored skin. All in all, a well-formed face.

Buck continues to regale them with talk for most of the night. It's revealed that he, a DJ, hosts a show—*Buck Wild in the Morning*—that is the second-most listened-to radio program in the Delta. "Right behind Mr. Paul Harvey," he says. An expert on country and western music, he speaks passionately about the Ryman Auditorium and the sad, misbegotten life of Hank Williams. "His wife—now that woman was something else!" His two favorite singers are Charley Pride and Dottie West. Because, he confesses, they sing mostly happy love songs. "The kind where it ends the way it should."

In between stories, he uncorks the malbec and pours it into two tall wineglasses. He passes one of them to Forney's mother, then raises his own above his head. "To Felicia," he says. "May her voice one day charm the millions as it has charmed me."

She smiles at this but appears embarrassed.

This pleases Forney, her embarrassment. He lifts his glass of milk, and says, "Here, here." Most of it's clear to him now anyway. His mother doesn't give two hoots about this strange little man; rather, she's using him for something. For his connections probably. That's it.

AFTER DINNER, they drift back outside to the front porch. The overhead lights are kept off, and the night hems in around them, alive with squalling bobwhites and the wet patter of rain. Forney dangles one arm off the edge of the porch into the night air, the slow drizzle soothing him.

Meanwhile, his mother and Buck are on the swing. They cast a strange silhouette in the shadows. Forney can't stand to look at them. He may as well be on a different planet. That's how far away he feels from them. He shouldn't care what they do. But he does care, and he *does* look back at them. Several times, in fact. And no matter how hard his stare, the darkness remains impenetrable. The only thing he can definitely make out is the steady *slick-slack* of the swing. Going back and forth.

Buck says, "Can I trouble you for something sweet?"

"There's some ice cream in the freezer." Forney's mother's voice is sleepy and thick. "Forney will get you a bowl."

Get? Forney's no fool. He understands they want him to get lost so they can have a moment of privacy. To perhaps kiss and bump up against each other, breathing hard. Do what adults do in these situations.

"I've got the most prodigious sweet tooth," Buck is saying now. Almost as an apology. "I just can't help myself."

"Okay, okay." Forney hurries off toward the kitchen. Using a dirty spoon, he scoops a fat gunk of ice cream into a cereal bowl. He returns as quietly as possible. Hoping to catch them in some kind of embarrassing act. What he plans on doing after such a discovery he's not sure. Maybe throw the ice cream at them, bowl and all. To his surprise, however, they have left the porch. He cuts on the lights, causing dirt daubers to zip by his ears and congregate around the glowing bulbs. He swats them away, the bowl of ice cream slipping from his fingers and shattering about his feet.

In the driveway, there are footsteps. Some whispers.

"You all right up there," comes a voice. Buck's voice.

Forney can see them then. They're standing beside the large green Crown Victoria. Buck's leaning against the driver's-side door, his skinny arms hitched around the rearview mirror for balance. Beside him, Forney's mother rests her head on the roof of the car, perhaps gazing at the stars. It's no longer raining, and the night has turned soft. Moonlight makes everything silvery and new looking.

They pass a cigarette between them, each taking long drags. When they finish, Buck crushes it under his shoe. He looks up at Forney on the porch, who's watching all of this in a kind of wonder, and smiles. He ambles, in his slow, limping fashion, toward the boy to say good night. It has gotten late, he says. Time for him to hit the road.

There's no mention of the ice cream puddle or the flies it's beginning to attract.

After settling into his car, Buck rolls down the window, and hollers, "I'll see you friends later."

His fingers sticky with ice cream, Forney waves as the car backs up, turns, and then trundles down their drive. Forney's mother remains in the front yard until the car has completely disappeared around the turn. She returns to the porch. Humming, half-heartedly, Tammy Wynette's "Take Me to Your World."

Forney says, "That man likes you."

"Think so?" She stoops and plucks broken shards of bowl from the gooey ice cream soup puddle. "What a mess, Forney. Jesus."

"He's your boyfriend?"

"Forney, *please,*" she says, and slings the broken pieces of bowl out into the bottomless night. "I'm tired of talking."

II.

The second time Buck Dickerson comes around, it's a Friday afternoon, and he's all business. He wants to get more acquainted with Felicia's voice, he says. And he decides they should move the piano into the living room from the hallway. "There," he claims, "the acoustics are better." Boxy and cumbersome, the upright piano once belonged to Forney's grandfather and somehow, through the years, found its way into their house. After they push the couch against the wall, they situate the piano in the center of the room, adding a metal folding chair in front of it.

Once seated, Buck rolls up his sleeves. "A little Debussy for our trouble." He lifts the lid and places his knotty fingers along the yellow keys. He plays. For the next few minutes, the most achingly beautiful sound envelopes the room. Forney and his mother are on the couch, silent. A little awed. Buck seems completely at home at the piano, his fingers plunk away at the keys with a slicing dexterity.

After he finishes, Forney's mother is breathless. She asks him for the name of the piece. Buck narrows his eyes at them. Looks disappointed. "Why," he says, "'Clair de Lune,' of course."

"Of course," she says, and closes her eyes, as if just remembering it. But Forney can hear the lie in her voice.

"Your turn," Buck says to her. He plays the beginning melody of Patsy Cline's "She's Got You."

Summoned, she rises from the couch and capers over. She tilts her face to the ceiling. Opens her mouth and out comes this voice—the purity of it shocks Forney. He's lost. Head spinning. So this is *her,* he finally understands.

An expert player, Buck unites the sound of the piano with her tone. The notes embrace her singing. Coils around the voice like a protective shield. The performance takes on a texture, a tangibility. Almost like Forney could reach up and catch the song in midair, feel the groves of it moving through his fingers as they passed by. *"I've got your class ring,"* his mother croons, *"that proved you cared."* The lyrics give him gooseflesh. It works a kind of voodoo on him. And his mother! She looks so young when she sings. She sways, her eyes still closed. Dad probably saw her this way years ago in Dallas: vulnerable, radiant with talent. This must be how other men see her, how Buck sees her now. Felicia. Forney rarely thinks of her first name. But now it comes to him over and over. Felicia, Felicia, Felicia. Not just his mother but a person, singular.

After the song, Buck turns to Forney, his eyes watery and wide. "See," he says to the boy. "See what your mama can do?"

And he does. He really does.

She practices with Buck late into the night, going through most of the Patsy Cline songbook, aptly ending the evening with "Sweet Dreams." Before he leaves, Buck kisses her hand. And this time Forney doesn't laugh.

ON FRIDAYS, Buck drives up in his outlandish car, pulls around back, and parks beside the unfinished chicken coop. He lopes through the back door, yapping like a grateful dog. "Weekend's here, friends," he bellows, and Forney and his mother run to meet him in the living room.

Not exaggerating about his sweet tooth, Buck usually brings some sugary confection for them to devour: cream-cheese Danishes, glazed bear claws, doughnut holes, strawberry crullers. You name it. And he always eats more than Forney and his mother, yet he remains rail thin. Puny almost.

No matter how late it is after practice, he never stays the night. Felicia and Buck maintain—at least in front of Forney—a professional, businesslike demeanor. Whatever occurs physically between them (and Forney tries to steer his brain away from such thoughts) is kept far from his purview. The only time they touch is just before Buck leaves, when he gallantly kisses her hand.

Most of their time together is devoted to singing. To improving her natural talents. Her voice is shaky in those first few sessions, unsure of itself. Buck, the patient teacher, shows her how to sing from her belly. How to use the air in her lungs and how to pace herself.

In most things, they agree. They quarrel, however, over song choice. She prefers the upbeat country pop melodies currently played on Top 40 radio. Songs such as "Meet Me in Montana" and "Lookin' for Love" and "Take Me Home, Country Roads." Buck will have none of it. He claims—and

Forney is apt to agree with him, though he never voices his opinion during the practices—those flimsy tunes will be forgotten in five years or so. "What you need," he argues, "is a more traditional sound." The achy-heart standards of years past. He steers her toward the likes of Loretta Lynn, Kitty Wells, and Lynn Anderson. Which she balks at. "They're all so whiney," she says, and Buck replies, confidently, that "whiney sells." Eventually, they compromise: Each practice session, they alternate between his song selections and hers.

Between songs, while she is gargling with whiskey to loosen up her vocal cords, Forney has several talks with Buck. Pleasant talks. He tells the boy about his failed marriage and his son who serves in the Peace Corps. "Somewhere off the coast of Africa," he says. "I'll show you on a map sometime." His ex-wife lives in Gatlinburg and works as a day performer at an amusement park called Silver Dollar City. "But that's all the past," he says, and then, in his deeper radio voice: "And we deal in futures."

Forney listens to Buck's radio show a couple of times during the week to see what it is like. Buck sounds like a much bigger man on the air. A learned man. He often gives brief history lessons on the music he's about to play. "Now this one here, friends," he says once, "was Bobbie Gentry's best-known and biggest hit to date. You might remember the TV movie inspired by the tune, starring teen heartthrob

Robby Benson." Then the music fades in as he says, "And don't forget: This is *Buck Wild in the Morning*!"

In late July, Forney's mother and Buck start gallivanting to clubs and piano bars with open-mic nights. Traveling to Biloxi and Tuscaloosa and Shreveport. "Fine-tuning our sound," Buck calls it. During these trips, Forney is always left with his father's brother and sister. "Those twins," his mother calls them. They still live together in their childhood home on Claymore Street in the nearby town. Aunt Mavis and Uncle Lucas pretend they don't care what his mother is up to, but Forney knows they are ravenous for what bits of information he can throw them. "Oh, her music teacher," he answers, when they ask about Buck. "Oh, really," they say, gazing at each other knowingly. As if he weren't even in the room. As if he were some kind of dummy and didn't know they were trying to pick him clean for information.

"He's teaching her how to sing is all," he offers.

"Sing what?"

"Country music."

"Of course he is."

THE TRIP TO MEMPHIS comes about in August. Buck drives up into the front yard one afternoon, the windows rolled down, radio blaring a David Allen Coe song. The

Crown Vic halts inches from the porch, its grille nosing the porch railing. "Easy now," Forney's mother hollers from the kitchen window. "You got the red ass or something?"

He's jabbering before he stumbles out of the car. "You won't believe it, friends," he says, gasping. "You simply won't believe it." An old friend who works at Capitol Records in Nashville as a talent scout called him up that morning. Bishop, the old friend, will be traveling to Memphis the following week to see an up-and-coming band at the Orpheum and wants to see Buck. "Shoot the shit" is how Buck put it. And Buck, seeing an opportunity, raved about this great female singer he knows who will be taking the stage at the Little Tina on Beale Street the night before.

"Who's that?" Forney asks.

"Her, friend." Buck nods to his mother.

"I didn't know you were going to Memphis?"

Forney's mother sips from her pink can of Tab. "Me either."

"Details, details," Buck tells them. "The point is: He said he'd drop by." Buck is panting now. "This is your moment, Bathsheba."

THEY GO SHOPPING in Jackson for a new outfit for Forney's mother. At McRae's and Gayfers, she dons various dresses. Spiriting out of the fitting rooms in gowns bathed in sparkles and flanked on either side by a fat shoulder pad. Buck says, "No, no, no" to all of them. "Understatement," he reminds her. "We want your voice to be onstage, not the dress." Eventually, they find one they both like: a modest green number with a silver belt.

"*Perfecto.*" Buck scoops up her hair in his hands. "We'll wear it up. Like this. Classic."

She's staring at her reflection in the three-paned dressing mirror. Her eyes settle on Forney sitting on a pink bench, studying a rack of women's lingerie. "Let's find something for him too. Something classic."

Buck agrees. They have decided to take Forney with them to Memphis. For the story. Play up the strong-widow-woman-turned-country-singer angle. Opry crowds eat that up, Buck says.

In JCPenney, Buck selects for Forney a gray suit with a starchy white button-up shirt. He was about to refuse the whole thing. *Thanks, but no thanks. I'll just stay behind with Aunt Mavis and Uncle Lucas.* But then his mother appeared behind him and pressed her fingers into his neck.

"For flourish," she says, and ties a blue bow tie around his neck. She guides him over to a full-length mirror. "Look at yourself: a little man."

Forney tells her the bow tie's choking him.

"It's supposed to choke you. Lets you remember what you're wearing is not some old potato sack."

The two of them—mother and son—gaze at the reflection of themselves wearing their new getups. *Like different people*, Forney thinks. Happier people. But is he happy? Or on the way to happiness? This singing stuff makes *her* happy, and he guesses he's happy that she's happy. But is he? The boy reflected back at him *appears* to be. While he's mulling this over, his mother kisses the top of his head. Normally, she's a side hugger at best. So this is like an atomic bomb to his senses.

"Who are we?" he asks.

She beams. "Whoever we goddamn want to be, sweetheart."

Sweetheart—he repeats it quietly. Savors the word in his mouth as if it were a Jolly Rancher.

Behind them, Buck's applauding.

FORNEY'S IN THE BACK SEAT of the Crown Vic on their way to Memphis. They stop at four gas stations along the highway, and each time Buck returns with individually wrapped fried pies or an assortment of candies. He munches as he drives.

"My god," Forney's mother says once when he tosses a box of Krispy Kremes between them. "You've got a problem." She averts her eyes as he licks the sweet crust from his fingers then dusts the crumbs from his lap.

"My nerves," he explains.

"He's coming to see me." She looks at him again. "Not you."

He cranks the Crown Vic, and Forney's happy to be moving again. Down Highway 51, the same highway that runs in front of Graceland. Which his mother points out several times, as if the coincidence were a good omen or something.

Forney has this notion that he'll see Memphis glittering in the distance a good mile or two before they reach it. So far, however, there's been nothing but a wide stretch of nothingness in front of and behind them: a hazy wall of humidity, a diminishing wall of trees. Like they're headed away from civilization, not toward it.

The air conditioner conks out soon after they pass Grenada, so they roll the windows down—but not before his mother wraps a scarf around her newly curled chignon. Buck keeps the radio on so loud that Forney can hear the music even above the roar of wind gushing in and out of the car. By the first note, Buck usually recognizes the song and—unable to squash his radio-host tendencies—shares his knowledge with the car. "The Statler Brothers," he yells over his shoulder to Forney. "'Too Much on My Heart.'" Or, later, to Forney's mother: "'I Wouldn't Change You If I Could,' Ricky Skaggs." Or to himself: "'There's No Gettin'

Over Me,' Ronnie Milsap," his eyes scanning over the empty road tarring over in the afternoon heat.

"You ever meet any of them?" Forney asks at one point. "The singers."

Buck catches Forney's eyes in the rearview mirror and winks. "Oh, I've got some connections. Here and there."

THEY PARK in a large three-story garage two blocks from the Little Tina. Scrunched in the back seat, Forney and his mother take turns changing into their new clothes. As before, he finds his suit oppressive. Stepping into the neon brilliance of Beale Street, he feels like he's got a wet towel around his chest. Buck finds a pay phone and calls the motel to inform them that they'll be late checking in, and in the meantime, Forney and his mother cross the street. She leads him to a tall statue situated in a little pavilion.

"W. C. Handy," she tells him, and touches the statue's foot. "For luck."

Forney places his hand on the other leg. "Okay," he says.

Buck finds them like this. "Ready?"

The Little Tina is a bar and grill of sorts, named—according to the placard outside—for an ill-fated (possibly fictitious) showboat that used to go up and down the Mississippi River, once upon a time. The restaurant's located in a redbrick storefront, stuffed between a dance hall and an old-timey general store with signage boasting the world's largest pair of overalls for sale. Buck leaves Forney and his mother at the front of the Little Tina to speak with a man standing behind the pedestal by the bar. He's dressed in some sort of costume that Forney can't place—a strange suitcoat, a funny hat, like a train conductor maybe. It's poorly lit, and Forney cannot see what lies beyond the bar, but he's excited. Finally, Buck waves them over, and they follow the man around the bar and down a long hallway, through a large crowd of people waiting in line, that empties into a dining room. Windows hold the illusion of the outside, showing segments of what must be a large mural of a riverbank, and brown slivers of trees and dark-green overgrowth. The waiters wear gray uniforms with bright yellow sashes. They are moving quickly about the room, gliding past one another in a kind of dance as they take orders, carry large trays of food, flip warm disks of corn bread from cast-iron skillets.

Their booth's in the back, half-hidden by a greasy cloud of cigarette smoke. On the walls surrounding them are portraits and drawings of the "famous" showboat, calling it a "Floating Theatre of Talent." Having swiped a menu earlier, Forney learns that the boat supposedly sunk sometime before the Civil War. There was a story about how this was the North's fault, but he couldn't follow the logic. Their waitress—a chubby girl with deep pockmarks on her face—brings them a plate of pickled onions and mugs of ice water. Not wasting any time, Forney's mother orders a gin and tonic. Buck and Forney ask for sweet teas.

A raised platform along with a microphone and an electric keyboard is at the center of the room. A skinny black man with an exuberant mass of dreadlocks is playing a saxophone while the people in the restaurant blissfully boo him. Even though, to Forney's ears, the man seems to be doing a good job.

"Tough crowd." His mother's hand finds his. Another first. He can hardly believe it: atomic bomb number two.

"Bishop said he'd be here by now," Buck is saying. He glances down at his wristwatch. "We're on in thirty—I think." He tells them that he needs to speak with the manager, give him the tape of recorded music she would be singing to. (Buck didn't feel confident enough in his ability to play tonight.)

The crowd's heckles grow louder, but the man on the saxophone appears oblivious. Forney catches the melody. "'Love Is Here to Stay,'" he says, but his mother's looking off and doesn't hear him. Last year, his school's music teacher showed them *An American in Paris*, and this particular piece he liked the best. The saxophonist finishes, and he bows. There is a rupture of applause then. Cheering him off the stage.

"Pearls before swine." Forney's mother gulps down her water. "Where's my gin and tonic?"

When Buck returns, he informs them of a problem. The manager is insisting that she take the stage next after a fifteen-minute intermission. Supposedly, they have a full list of performers. "Says he needs to keep it moving." Buck shakes his head, clearly disgusted with the way things are turning out. "Just get up there," he finally says. "It'll be better this way. He'll see you in medias res. Give you a chance to work out the nervousness."

Forney grips his mother's wrist. "If they boo you, just keep on singing."

She examines the crowd. A mix of tourists and locals. Shoveling fried catfish in their mouths. "Bastards." She gently slaps herself across the face. "Let's do this."

Forney watches as Buck takes her to the stage and helps her onto the platform. The restaurant lights dim, and the crowd, curious, becomes silent and turns their attention to the woman onstage before them. The floodlights pick up the green in her dress and the silver of the belt—she is, indeed, dazzling. Forney wishes she could see herself like this. Buck, the old fool, was right about everything: the dress, the hair. Forney's mother belonged there. In front of an audience. A hand unclenches from around his heart—he can feel the slow release. Maybe he's always loved his mother, and it has taken the singing and Buck and whatever else to awaken him to it. He recognizes it, this love inside him, and shudders. With this feeling of love comes, also, dread. Dread because when you love someone you put yourself in their hands. Give them the power to destroy you with something as little as a look. Or a song.

From the speakers in the wall, Buck's sure-footed piano riffs of Kitty Wells's "It Wasn't God Who Made Honkey Tonk Angels" floods the room. His mother waits for the moment. Parts her lips.

She sings.

And nothing happens.

The audience returns to their plates of coleslaw and fried dill pickles and steaming lumps of turnip greens. They continue with their loud talk, as if his mother were nothing more than a noisy bird on a windowsill. Forney can't believe it. Boos would have been better.

Buck comes back to the booth. "Bishop will be here soon."

But Forney hardly hears him. Loud sobs are shaking loose from his throat.

III.

One balmy summer day, they were outside shelling peas, their hands stained purple, when Forney's father keeled over, landing facedown in the monkey grass. At first his mother thought it was just the heat. He had merely passed out. "You, Reuben," she kept saying, nudging him with her foot, placing her ear to his chest. When she discovered he wasn't breathing, she leaped inside and called 911. Forney put his father's head in his lap and slapped his cheeks. Neither one of them knew CPR, so all they could do was wait for the ambulance. Keep the ants off of him. "Reuben, Reuben," his mother kept repeating. Like a chant. Forney, on the other hand, didn't say anything. He didn't cry either—though no one would have blamed him if he had. But no: His sockets remained dry even during the memorial service, even when he saw the little urn being handed to his mother that contained—somehow—the remains of his father, all that he had been, all that he would ever be. So, needless to say, it's a great shock to him that he decides to let loose with the tears when he does. Here, at the Little Tina.

His mother sings two more songs and quietly exits the stage to little fanfare. Two hours later, Buck's friend Bishop turns up. A tall man with frumpy hair and a curlicue mustache that curves into itself like a musical note. By this time, Forney has taken off his coat and undone the bow tie. The swirl in his mother's chignon has become knotted. Buck nibbles a lemon. Their hands are slimy from all the catfish they've eaten.

Bishop moseys up to the table. “Who died?”

“You’re late.” Forney’s mother is on her third gin and tonic.

Buck spits out a seed. “You missed it B. She was—spectacular.”

Bishop slides into Forney’s side of the booth. The waitress appears and asks him what he would like to drink. Bishop studies Forney’s mother. “I’ll have what the pretty lady is having.”

She huffs, clearly unimpressed.

Wiping his hands, Buck boasts about her performance. To hear him tell it, she rallied the crowd with her voice. He’s so convincing, in fact, that Forney begins to wonder if it happened just as he said.

“Do an encore?” Bishop asks her.

Buck stammers. “Other performers were in the wings—didn’t want to be rude.”

“Rude? Nothing’s rude in show business,” Bishop says.

He gazes at the stage, which is empty now.

There were several performers after Forney’s mother—some horrible, a few mediocre, but none as good as the saxophonist. Or his mother. He’s not about to say that though. Forney’s had enough of this music business. He may never listen to another song for as long as he lives.

“Let’s get up there,” Bishop says. “What’s stopping us?”

“Huh?” Forney’s mother asks.

Bishop admits he can play the piano if she's willing. "To make up for being late." He swipes her gin and tonic, and finishes it with one deep gulp.

"Now wait a minute," Buck is saying, but it's too late. Forney can tell that some kind of energy has passed between Bishop and his mother. Forney and Buck have been excluded from the conversation.

Bishop inquires about what songs she sang tonight, and after she tells him, he huffs, "Those dreary things! What you need is something fiery. Full of spunk."

One of her eyebrows arches. "Exactly."

"And your hair," he goes on, waving his hands as he speaks. "The updo doesn't help anyone."

Laughing, she undoes the rest of her ratty bob.

Buck stands. "I think we should ask for the check when the girl comes back. Forney looks tired."

"I do?"

Forney's mother says that she has come all this way for this man—meaning Bishop—to hear her sing and, by god, she is going to.

Bishop interrupts her. "I've got the perfect song too."

"Oh, yeah?"

He sings a little of it, his voice husky and out of tune: "*She's forty-one and her daddy still calls her baby . . .*"

"You got to be kidding me." Buck rips open a packet of sugar and pours it down his throat.

BISHOP AND FORNEY'S MOTHER perform Tanya Tucker's "Delta Dawn." Half-drunk, she slurs most of the words. Bishop, accompanying her on the keyboard, harmonizes during the chorus. The rowdy crowd at the Little Tina has dwindled down to mostly drunks, and a few beefy men catcall her during the song. Afterward, everyone applauds except for Buck and Forney.

Bishop and Forney's mother lock arms and bow. Bishop stoops so low in his bow that his hairpiece flops to the floor, revealing a shiny bald head. At this, the crowd becomes ecstatic in their applause. A few even stand.

Forney's confused. "What's happening?"

"Nothing," Buck says, "but the utter downfall of mankind."

Afterward, his mother returns to the table, shiny with sweat. She slides in beside her son this time, nodding at a couple of flannel-clad men who hoot at her from another table.

"Most fun I've had in a long time," says Bishop, taking the place beside Buck. He begins to readjust his toupee, but she stops him.

"I like it—natural." She rubs his naked scalp, as if it were a crystal ball.

Forney announces he's ready to go.

"Here." His mother unloops Forney's bow tie from his collar, then wraps it around her head to keep the hair out of her face.

"Attractive," Buck says.

"Says the man with the body."

Bishop places his arm around Buck's shoulder. "That's my friend you're talking about." He and Forney's mother share a laugh.

Buck looks at Forney: His eyes say, *Help*. But what can he do? Buck's the adult; he's just a boy. Just a fatherless boy in a strange city. Surrounded by strange people. For the first time in his life, he longs for the farmhouse. The middle of nowhere. The inside of his closet.

"I think I'm too young for all of this," Forney says, and Bishop and his mother laugh even louder.

"A toast," his mother says. "To friend Buck! And to friend Bishop!"

"Yes!" Bishop raises his glass. "To all those who wish us well—and those who don't can go to hell!"

"To hell!" she agrees.

What occurs next surprises everyone at the table, especially Forney. His body knows what to do before his brain does. Or, at least, it seems to happen this way. He can see his hand grip his half-filled glass of sweet tea. He can see his hand raise it and then sling it at Bishop. Hard. The glass pops the side of the man's head, splashing him, and then ricochets off the table onto the floor. He's drenched. An ice cube rests, miraculously, atop his head. "You bastard," Bishop mumbles. He lurches across the table and snags Forney's collar.

His mother screams. And Buck, in a feat of acrobatics, twists around Bishop and puts the bigger man in a headlock. Bishop releases Forney at once, and the two men fall back to their side of the booth.

The waitress returns. "Fucking rednecks," she says, and tosses the bill on the table.

WHILE BISHOP'S GONE to the bathroom to clean up, Forney's mother proclaims it's time, at last, to leave. They shuffle to their feet and walk outside into the steamy night.

"I'll be on directly," she says, waving them away, and it dawns on Buck and Forney at the same time because they both say "No" in unison.

She gapes at them. "I need to stay behind and smooth over what Junior here did."

"Smooth over?" Buck says. "Smooth over how?"

She smiles. Lipstick stains her teeth. "Easy, cowboy. I'm just going to talk some more with him—like you said, he can help me. Us."

Buck says that he doesn't feel right about her staying behind.

"I'm not asking permission."

"Tell her, Forney." Buck looks to the boy once again for salvation. "Tell your mother how you want her to come back with us."

Please, Forney wants to say, but he knows better. He says, instead: "I don't care what she does."

THE PLACE THEY'RE STAYING AT is called the Hunk-a-Hunk-of-Burning-Love Motel and Diner. Elvis memorabilia litters the cramped room: a movie poster from *Blue Hawaii* plastered over the closet door, vinyl records lined against the walls. The beds are shaped like guitars. Forney falls onto one of them and buries his face in a bright red pillow. Using the phone on the table by the TV, Buck calls room service and orders something, then he comes over and nudges Forney with his knee.

"I want to show you this," he says.

Forney sits up.

Buck pulls out a folded sheet of paper from his back pocket. On the other bed, he proceeds to unfold it with great care until it covers half the mattress. Forney scoots over for a better look: It's a map, yellowed and crumbly. All of the countries are faded pastels. Buck points to the salmon-colored blob of Africa. "This is where my boy is," he says. "Tolliver." But he's not pointing at Africa after all but off to the side of it at a scattering of dots Forney has to squint to see. "Cape Verde."

Buck yawns and sits beside Forney on the bed. He smells of talcum powder and spearmint. "My son says he wants to be a poet. Can you believe that? I didn't know people decided to be poets." He sighs, and when he relaxes his face, Forney can see the man's sadness, the pureness of it. He wants to look away and does when Buck says, "Thought it just happened to them, or something, like a car wreck."

Forney kicks off his shoes and goes to the bathroom to pee. Above the toilet, there's a picture of fat Elvis in a bedazzled jumpsuit. Under it, the caption reads: EVERY KING DESERVES A THRONE. The map is gone when he returns, and Buck lies prone on the bed, his arm covering his eyes.

"If someone can decide to be a singer," he mumbles, "then I suppose somebody can decide to be a poet too."

There's a knock on the door. Both jump, but they know it couldn't be Forney's mother come back to them. "Room service," a voice trills from the other side. Buck opens the door, and in trots this old woman with orangey clown hair, wearing a poodle skirt. On a silver tray, she carries a steamy cinnamon bun, glistening in pearly white frosting. Buck takes the tray from her and pays in cash.

With a plastic knife, Buck saws into the pastry. Making two flakey pieces. "Here," he says, dumping one slice on a napkin, then handing it over to Forney. They eat in silence and keep their ears trained to the noises outside, but they are not fools. They suspect she won't be back until morning. Maybe later. But for now, they share a cinnamon bun and the ridiculous hope that she might return to them before they finish.

The old woman takes her time in leaving them. "You boys be good now," she says, probably thinking—Forney is sure of it—*This is the saddest room in the universe.*

THE EXAGGERATIONS

When I was fourteen, Uncle Lucas decided to take me to a bachelor party. His longtime friend Buddy Cooper was getting married. Buddy Cooper was a real-life cowboy: wore Wranglers and thick-heeled boots and a stiff Stetson hat. He smelled like fresh hay, but his hands were always impossibly clean. During the summer, Uncle Lucas would sometimes drive me out to Buddy Cooper's farm two counties over in Itta Bena to ride horses and fish for brim in his pond. He was a nice man and got along in a good humor with Uncle Lucas, staying up late into the night on those visits to retell old stories of their past exploits together. Their voices, I remember, were soft and measured with each other—like the whispery *crick-crack* of old tree limbs being nudged apart by wind—and it was easy to fall asleep listening to them talk in the other room.

One thing you should know about Uncle Lucas: He liked to exaggerate. His talent was taking ordinary events, the everyday happenings of life, and giving them that spark they needed in order to become memorable, even remarkable. Dressed in the finest of tweed suits, he would regale those who shopped in his department store on the square in town with one story after another, stories about the locals whom nobody remembered exactly but were somehow still faintly known. He had the confidence and air of a learned historian even though—if Aunt Mavis was right—he had barely graduated from high school.

But with Buddy Cooper, my uncle never exaggerated. The truth of their memories together was a sacred thing to him. I never questioned Uncle Lucas about this because I thought it had something to do with their friendship, the bond between them. The fatherless boy that I was, I knew very little about the world of men and what kept them in healthy fellowship with one another.

Aunt Mavis did not like the idea of my tagging along for the bachelor party, especially when she understood where it was taking place. "Fay's," she hollered. But Uncle Lucas told her that I was old enough to know "some things about this world," and after he said this, she looked at me as if she had never seen me before. Said if I went I'd be disappointing my parents who had entrusted me to their care.

"Hardy har har," Uncle Lucas said to this. "If his daddy

was still living, he would have done took him. And his mother—well, his mother—" That was a tender subject, my mother, so Aunt Mavis held up her hand to silence him.

"Fine," she said. "I hope you both get so sot drunk your livers turn black and fall out your back ends." At this, she turned on her heels and huffed up the stairs to her room.

After she had slammed the door, I asked Uncle Lucas if that could really happen, your liver turning black and falling out, and he said, "Naw," but then he seemed to ponder the thought for a few seconds more and said, in a more serious tone, "At least I don't think so."

THE ONE UNCLE LUCAS used to tell me all the time was about the little girl and her pig. According to Uncle Lucas, the girl was the only child of a dirt farmer, and her parents spoiled her, gave her anything she wanted. And what she wanted one year, at the age of twelve, was to be crowned Little Miss Farm Special at the Mid-Mississippi State Fair. All she needed was a pig. The competition consisted of the contestants, dressed in fine puffy gowns, parading their fattest hog out onto the muddy fairgrounds. They were scored on their attire, their poise, and—of course—their pig.

The girl's father cashed out his Christmas Club and bought her a piglet from the man whose fields he worked. The girl tended to the animal all summer long, feeding it cow milk and thick triangles of corn bread and, later, expensive bags of feed to fatten it up. At night, before bed, she would sit on the back porch with the pig's knotty snout in her lap and rub baby oil into its tender flesh. She named the pig Suzanne, and on the day of the competition, the animal was a behemoth, its skin the color of eggnog and its curlicue tail adorned with an elegant blue bow. To complete the look, the girl wore a matching ribbon in her own hair, and they trotted out onto the fairgrounds, expecting to win the day. Unbeknownst to her, however, it was against the rules to doll pigs up with ribbons, the judges preferring pigs to retain a more natural look, and they were disqualified. To make matters worse, Suzanne had gained a multitude of hungry admirers during her first outing in public. By the time the girl and the pig had made it back to the parking lot, her father—who was angry because of all the money he'd wasted on such a venture—had already sold Suzanne off to the man who owned the local meat locker.

Needless to say, the girl pitched some kind of a fit when the man came to take Suzanne away. The animal, sensing the girl's distress, squealed and squealed, roiling its great body back and forth as the man led her off. The girl cried and moaned the whole way home, her dress all bunched up around her in the tiny truck cab like a glittery cloud. Her father regretted what he had done, but he'd made back the money he lost from his Christmas Club twice over and promised her he'd use it to get her a new pet. "A real one this time," he said. "A pedigreed dog." At this, the girl cried louder. That night, while her parents were asleep, she slid out of her bedroom window and rode her bicycle all the way across town to the meat locker. The building made a crooked shadow in the night sky, and she was almost too frightened to enter, but she pressed on. There, in a pen beside the rusted meat hooks, she found Suzanne, oinking and snorting, still alive, mingling with a drove of other hogs. "So she set them all aloose," Uncle Lucas would say. "And there are still feral pigs up in the woods that owe their lineage to that girl."

Here, he would end the story, and though I was young, I knew an embellishment when I heard one, knew my uncle could stretch the truth so thin that you could read the newspaper through it. But that didn't matter much—not to me, at least—when it came to enjoying it for its beauty and humor. Uncle Lucas's exaggerations had a pull to them, drawing me (and perhaps others) closer and closer to something else, something underneath the story, something that he was trying to communicate indirectly. It wasn't that he attempted to drop morals in with his exaggerations, I don't think, or give life lessons exactly, like the parables of Jesus. No, what he was doing with his storytelling was trying to shape the world into something better than it was. In his heart, I don't think he could face the finalities of life—unexplainable death, loss of love, petty hates and injustices—and so, in memory, he colored events differently. Growing up, I was constantly at war with myself: You see, I knew it was foolish to believe a word he said when he got going on one of his long talks, but that didn't stop me from desperately wanting to.

HIS LISTENERS KNEW he made up most or all of what he told them, but they forgave him because he was not of them, and I think they found it charming that he took such an interest in their town lore. None of my family was ever considered a part of town; our roots were not deep enough. Fifty years ago, my widower grandfather left his fledgling law practice and moved to Mississippi, bringing with him his three children—Uncle Lucas; Uncle Lucas's twin sister, Mavis; and his older brother, Reuben (my father)—to start a new life in this state, where the cost of living was cheap and good lawyers were sparse.

My family hailed from Illinois, and in the Delta, that might as well have been the moon. Here, even when I was growing up in the 1980s, it's all about family and who's kin to whom; here, girls are given double names—Anna-Taylor, Hattie-Frank, Sarah-Burden—so that people will know who their mothers had been before they were married; here, you say you live in "God's Country" because the endless fields of soybeans and rice and cotton that separate your cluster of a town from other towns gives you this feeling of importance, of significance, that you might matter, that surely God can't miss you if you are one of only a few looking up at him. But in my family, we didn't believe in God, so when we glanced above our heads, all we saw was blue sky, ozone, the faint scars of cloud.

MY FAVORITE EXAGGERATION was the one Uncle Lucas told about me. During the summers, I would sometimes go with him to his store to help fold and arrange the new shipments of polo shirts and trousers. When people would come in, he'd sometimes point at me, and say, "There's my nephew. He's going to be famous one day. He's special." Then he'd wink at me like what he had said was gospel.

He knew I liked to write, to tell my own stories just like he did, and made it up in his mind that I was going to be a well-known writer. "Another Hemingway! A Faulkner—only my nephew will make some damn sense!" It felt good to live in the warmth of his imagination; however, the truth was a little closer to earth. Each of my stories—if you could call them that—was barely a page long, a sketch of description or a stray thought captured in my own paltry grasp of language, and Aunt Mavis, who was also my seventh grade English teacher, said I had a problem sticking to my subject: "You wander and wander and digress so much," she wrote once in the margins of one of my themes. "It's like trying to find a story in a hurricane."

But my uncle told me all the greats were misunderstood in their own time. He said, "Forney Culpepper. Now that is a name that should be on the cover of a book." And every now and then, I almost believed him. Then my mother would send me a letter from Nashville, telling me about the musicians she was about to go on tour with and how, in just a year or two, she would hit the big time and fly me out to live with her. That brought me down real quickly. My mother's letters reminded me who I really was: I was Forney, the boy whose father was dead and whose mother had left him to pursue a far-flung singing career; I was Forney, named for a nowhere town in Texas, where two people who barely knew each other conceived me. Truth: Forney Culpepper was not really that special at all. Ultimately, I could never keep up the exaggerations of my uncle for long—sooner or later, I always gave in to the rough way of things.

THE JUKE JOINT, unofficially called Fay's, was affixed to the bank of the Yalobusha River not twenty yards from where the train tracks crossed over the water on a rickety bridge. Because the county was dry, Fay's was, for the longest time, one of the few places near town where a man could wet his whistle in peace away from the company and influence of his wife. You had to walk to get there; most of the men parked their trucks on the side of a gravel road and trekked to the shack, using the river or the train rails to guide them. It would be naïve to assume the police didn't know about Fay's, but since most of their own fathers had frequented the establishment, they let it alone so long as there wasn't any trouble.

Who Fay had been was long forgotten by the time Uncle Lucas took me there, but on our way that night to the bachelor party, he told me the story of her, or rather his story *for* her. She had once owned a bed-and-breakfast in town called the Redbud Inn and often kept girls there on the payroll for the men's pleasure. "It was a good business in those days," Uncle Lucas said. "Fay had a nice setup, and the men adored her." She had a shock of bright red hair, and when she traipsed up and down the square, the women would cross the street to avoid her. Some would even hiss.

As my uncle tells it, Fay messed up and got herself pregnant, and when the news of the pregnancy leaked, the fine ladies of that time turned mean. Fay could claim, they feared, just about any of their husbands as the father. In great distress, the ladies met at the café on the square to discuss what to do about her; of course, the meeting was done in secret, under the guise of a monthly gathering of the local chapter of the Daughters of the American Revolution. After two hours of debating the issue of Fay and her illegitimate child, it was decided that the woman must be run out of town, plain and simple, and since the menfolk were too dazzled by her to think straight, they would have to do it themselves.

"That very night they went to the Redbud Inn," Uncle Lucas said. "And the whole herd of them—respectable church ladies in frilly dresses and fancy flowered hats—went to her front door." Looking out her window from the second floor, Fay observed the mob approaching and told one of her girls to latch the doors. She then opened her window and called down to them, asking if they had followed their husbands to come see what all the fuss was about. She laughed at the women, shooed them home, but the ladies, indignant from her laughter, would not be moved. Fay had underestimated them.

Back then, it was high fashion to smoke, so many of them had their cigarette lighters in their purses, and a few of the ladies even had, on their person, matches. The thought must have occurred to them in one grand moment of inspiration: Smoke her out. "No one knows who started the fire, but once lit, the house took like kindling." The flames lapped up the delicately painted siding, engulfing the pretty inn and driving out the girls. The ladies circled the house like a coven of witches and caught them, one by one, as they came running out in their silk nightdresses. "You could hear the screams echoing through town." But the one the ladies wanted most of all remained inside; she had phoned the fire department and the police, and held firm that they would rescue her in time, but the fire worked faster than she anticipated, forcing her to the roof, where she clung to the chimney until the Redbud Inn caved in on itself.

The ladies scattered as the bed-and-breakfast came tumbling down. "It is said," Uncle Lucas told me, "that many of them couldn't ever wash the smoke out of their hair and that they smelled of soot for the rest of their days." Amazingly, the way he tells it, Fay had more life in her than the ladies of the town gave her credit for because, miracle of miracles, she survived. Firemen found her smoking body amid the ruins and carried her in secret to an old bachelor doctor out in the country. There she was nursed back to health and ended up, in the end, having that baby, a girl.

Fearing their wives, the men built Fay a small house deep in the woods. "She lived out the rest of her life in relative peace there," Uncle Lucas said. When she died, the men returned to the house to pay their respects and found the daughter, now grown, who could have been any of theirs, cooking corn liquor on the back porch as if she had been expecting them. "She offered them a snort of it. And they each took some and toasted Fay." Thus, it became tradition for many of them to meet once or twice a month at

Fay's, drink the daughter's moonshine, and as the train rustled past at midnight, hold their drinks in the air and, in a solemn chorus, roar, "To Fay!"

ALTHOUGH THEY WERE TWINS, Uncle Lucas and Aunt Mavis looked nothing alike. Uncle Lucas had the same blunt nose and wide mouth that my father had. Aunt Mavis, on the other hand, possessed the narrow face and delicate features of a French aristocrat.

In her college days at Ole Miss, she fancied herself something of a poet. She wrote her senior thesis on Marianne Moore and Elizabeth Bishop, and had plans of attending graduate school, but after graduation, my grandfather suddenly died, so she stayed behind "to see about things" for a while. Twenty years later and she was still seeing about things and remained single.

Uncle Lucas never married either, and for most of their lives, they lived together in the same house on Claymore Street, and I lived with them during my teenage years while my mother was away. I remember, before she left me with them, that she told me to be kind to my aunt and uncle because I was all they had left in the world and, besides, I wouldn't have to stay with them long anyway, just until she got herself settled in Nashville. I was ten, and four years later, around the time of the bachelor party, I wouldn't have left them for anything. We were, for better or worse, a family. We had long dinners together, where Aunt Mavis and I listened to Uncle Lucas go on in his usual manner. We saw plays and ballets in Jackson at Thalia Mara Hall, took weekend vacations to Biloxi and Memphis and New Orleans. All this time, I considered us outsiders—not just in the town, but in life itself, and a certain closeness developed among the three of us, an intimacy the likes of which I'd never known.

Now I see that this business about being outsiders was perhaps more complicated than I'd first imagined. I think we knew, on some instinctual level, that we could never be like them, the rest of the town, and likewise, they didn't see any reason for trying life our way. The town, for the most part, was hunkered down in the insular culture of Little League and church and bunko, and though there is, to my mind, nothing especially wrong with that, our interests lay elsewhere. In a place where every household seemed to have a garden, we kept our lawn bare and preferred the comforts of the indoors where, during the hot months—July and August and sometimes September—we'd spend the long sweltering afternoons reading, cushioned from the heat by a loud AC unit my grandfather had bought at Sears many years ago. We were always reading something. Stacks of books—more like walls of them—lined the hallways and covered the dining-room table and propped open doors. Aunt Mavis mainly read volumes of poetry while Uncle Lucas and I devoured novels, the trashier the better. One summer we made our way through the complete works of Miss Jacqueline Susann (Aunt Mavis, of course, had no idea). Some nights my aunt and uncle would get a wild hair and read passages from Shakespeare or Auden aloud. Both of them had rich, thick voices—a mix of Midwestern flatness and Southern drawl—that had a way of lifting me right off my seat. It was almost as entertaining as my uncle's exaggerations.

It didn't take me long to hear the rumors about my aunt and uncle, that there was something funny about the way they never married and still lived together. I had a violent streak back then and would fight any of the kids at school who so much as hinted in my presence what their parents had whispered about at home, that Uncle Lucas and Aunt Mavis were somehow incestuous. This was an exaggeration that Uncle Lucas couldn't control, and the truth was much more pedestrian than the town's imagination. My aunt and uncle were creatures of habit, and the habit of living together had seemed more preferable than being alone. They were, after all, friends, knowing each other better than anyone else, and they accepted the faults of the other as easily as could be expected of twins and siblings who were believers and practitioners of unconditional love.

Soon after the bachelor party, my uncle left us. He

moved to the little room above his store, and Aunt Mavis, I think, was hurt, but understood his reasons even better than I did at the time.

THE MEN IN MY FAMILY had one thing in common: bad hearts. Each of them died from some kind of heart condition, and it was always unexpected. "We just fall dead," Uncle Lucas was wont to say. Aunt Mavis found my grandfather slouched over his desk one morning, already purple and cold. My father and I were shelling peas when his heart quit working and he went tumbling off the back deck. And Uncle Lucas was in Canada when his time came. I was a junior in high school. He had gone to a convention in Toronto, his first and only time traveling outside the country. On his last night there, he ate an elephant burger at an exotic restaurant, ice-skated at the park near his hotel, and braved a roller coaster that went upside down three times inside a mall the size of our town. Afterward, he wandered back to his hotel, perhaps drunk with the possibility of life, and fell asleep on top of the neatly made bed in his room. Sometime in the night, his forty-seven-year-old heart stalled. The news came to us at breakfast. A long-distance call and our troupe of three dwindled to two. Aunt Mavis had a time getting his body flown back to us.

AFTER PARKING AND WALKING for a while in the dark woods, Uncle Lucas and I finally reached the little clapboard house by the river. Even in moonlight, I could see how the woods had all but taken over Fay's. Kudzu and sumac pushed up through the floorboards on the little porch, and the roof sagged in the middle as if the house had taken one last great breath and then had given up altogether. We entered through the side door, which, for all I know, was the only door there was. The plastic floor bubbled and popped under our feet as we sallied past a row of card tables and made our way to a makeshift bar at the back of the dim room. There was no electricity. Greasy kerosene lanterns provided the light.

Uncle Lucas told the girl behind the bar he wanted two gin and tonics. The girl's eyes passed from his face to mine and then back again. She looked to be not much older than I was. A pale, thin girl, missing most of her bottom teeth. I wondered if this was supposed to be Fay's daughter, but I couldn't tell if she had her mother's flaming red hair or not because she kept it all bunched up underneath a dirty handkerchief wrapped about her head.

"Drink this," Uncle Lucas said, sliding a glass of clear liquid over to me. It looked like Sprite, and I took a long, desperate swig. The walk had dried me out. The drink tasted bitter and wrong, and I was able to choke down only a little. "Easy," he said. "Sip it. Will protect you from the mosquitoes."

He took his glass from the bar and went over to the tables, where a few men had already gathered for the evening. I wasn't sure what was supposed to happen here. I had a feeling that the men would drink and talk and maybe play cards, but I also wondered if something darker might occur. Perhaps Fay's still had those girls in silk nightgowns. I glanced back at the one behind the bar and shivered. She appeared to be the only one working tonight. At the time, I knew the basics of sex, what went where, but I couldn't imagine doing that with someone like her, someone I barely knew.

As the gathering of men grew, my uncle migrated from table to table, patting backs, laughing. I stayed put and felt out of place, like I was somehow intruding where I had no business. "You look scared," the girl said between puffs from a cigarette. I glanced back at her and took another sip of my drink, which began to taste better. Her dark eyes didn't seem to miss a bit of me, examining every part of my person with extreme scrutiny. "Guppy," she said, coming to some conclusion, and exhaled a large cloud of smoke.

I turned away. Around me, on the walls, hung the expressionless heads of fallen deer. Most of them were bucks, their knotty antlers twisting out of their skulls and touching the low-hanging ceiling. A thick skein of dust covered their glassy eyes. It wasn't long before I asked the girl if I could have another drink.

Two hours later, I was still there at the bar, nursing my fourth gin and tonic and feeling as if the world were fading away into a shapeless mass of color and sound. "Am I drunk?" I asked her, and she grinned, her toothless mouth now a warm invitation. "I could kiss your face off," I said, and this made her cackle uncontrollably.

About that time, Buddy Cooper, the groom, appeared at the side door. "Gentlemen," he announced to the gathering of men. "I've come to sow my last wild oat."

The men cheered, and catching on, I cheered too, longer and louder than the rest of them. He heard me at the back of the room and came over, a puzzled look on his face.

"Cowboy," I said to him. "What do you know?"

He took the drink from my hand and asked if I knew the whereabouts of my uncle.

"Over there," I said, pointing to a larger table where most of the men had congregated. "Talking shit."

"So dark in here. Can't see nothing." He smelled my drink and then noticed the girl over my shoulder. "Suppose this is real entertaining, huh?"

"Seems like he's having a good time," she said. "Guppy said he was a big boy now."

"I am a *big* boy," I said.

Taking my arm, he led me to the table where my uncle sat red-faced and laughing. "You need to cool off," Buddy Cooper said, and he produced a chair out of what seemed like thin air. "Here," he told me. "Pop a squat."

He had placed my chair slightly away from the table, out of the way. No one took any notice of my presence, and my uncle continued to hold court with the men. Buddy Cooper crossed his arms, half-smiling, and walked closer to the sound of Uncle Lucas's voice. When he joined the table, it became hard for me, in the shadowy light, to tell Buddy Cooper from the others. I only made out my uncle, rapt in the telling of his story. It was quite a sight. The men seemed to forget that he was Lucas Culpepper and accepted him completely as one of them, which made my heart sink. I felt abandoned. I wanted him to recognize me sitting there, facing him. I wanted him to call me over and introduce me to everyone. But that never happened. Instead, I sat there allowing the gin and loneliness to wash through me. The floor wobbled back and forth, and I had this crazy idea that the shack had detached from the side of the sandbar somehow and was floating us down the river. I gripped the edges of my chair to steady myself. After a while, the floor stopped moving, and I was all right again. I leaned forward in my chair to listen to Uncle Lucas speaking and realized that he was telling the gathering about Dr. Rosamond.

Dr. Rosamond, many years ago, tried to have his way with this married woman. He wrote her love songs, and on the weeks her husband wasn't home (he worked offshore), the doctor sang to her at night outside her window, his voice accompanied by his homemade git-fiddle. The way Uncle Lucas told it, the doctor burned for her with an achy, persistent kind of lust. And one day, enough was enough: He'd have her or die trying. In broad daylight, he kicked in her screen door and forced himself inside. She fought and screamed something good, and—lo!—the husband came home early and found the doctor bent over his wife trying to make time. The husband broke it up, but the doctor, crazy and slobbering all over himself, told the husband that he wasn't leaving. "You'll just have to kill me," Dr. Rosamond said.

The husband, not being one to fool around with, went to the bedroom and retrieved his double-barrel twelve gauge. He placed the gun square over Dr. Rosamond's chest and told him to leave the premises; otherwise, he would have the right to protect his family and blow him, medical degree and all, straight to hell's gates. Dr. Rosamond, who liked to see things through, clicked his heels together, pulled back his shoulders, and began to sing one of his woebegone love songs. He had made it to the chorus when the husband, frustrated and ready for dinner, pulled both triggers, emptying twin barrels of buckshot into the doctor's chest. “Shot his heart into a million bits,” Uncle Lucas was telling them. “And now his ghost, it is said, haunts the town, looking for pieces of it, his lost heart.”

“It was a poet’s death,” said one of the men, and the others laughed at him and begged Uncle Lucas for another story. My uncle glowed with benevolence and gestured for them to quiet down. Then a man with a handlebar mustache spoke up over the rest.

“That’s not how I heard it,” he said. His gaze traveled the length of the table, making a point to look each man in the eye, even me. “That’s not the way I heard it at all.”

Uncle Lucas sat back in his chair and studied the man. “Well,” he said to him. “That’s the only way I know it.” I nodded and wanted to tell the man with the shiny mustache that I’d heard about Dr. Rosamond for as long as I could remember. My uncle usually told it on Halloween, and it hadn’t changed much over the years. I stood, ready to speak, when Buddy Cooper came out of nowhere and shoved me back into my chair.

“You’ve had enough there, Bert,” he said, speaking to the man with the mustache. “You know you always go sour when you drink that dark liquor.”

The man told Buddy Cooper to shut his mouth, and his voice had changed, gotten deeper. The racket hushed. Everyone gazed at their drinks. I shivered all over in the new quiet. "Way I hear it," Bert went on, "it was his pecker that got shot off." He pointed at me and hissed. "You hear me, boy? Changed him from a gamecock to a hen."

Some of the men chuckled, but Buddy Cooper and I, loyal to my uncle, remained silent. Finally, after a long pause when everyone seemed to be trying to figure out what to do next, Uncle Lucas spoke: "Everyone knows it was, in fact, his heart." He drank what was left in his glass. "I don't like the way of that story you tell one bit."

More silence followed, then the sound of men shifting in their chairs.

Bert fingered his mustache, itched it for a while, and then grinned. Over the years, I would come to see other people give grins like that one: a hateful, cold smile. "I've heard many a story about you, Lucas Culpepper." He stood and turned, and I thought he was looking at me, but no: He looked at Buddy Cooper who stood beside me. "Have heard many stories that I don't spec I'd like repeated if it were me and I's unmarried."

Someone flipped the table, and I slid out of my chair, landing on my back, and didn't see any of what happened next. I heard yells. A slap. A hard, bone-deep thump. I jumped back to my feet but was still blinded from the commotion by a pair of tall shoulders. Then some of the men moved out of my way, and I saw that Buddy Cooper held Bert in a brutal headlock, the man's face turning all shades of red and purple, his mustache flapping about his mouth as if it were trying to fly off to safer territory.

Uncle Lucas stood behind them, speaking in a low voice to Buddy Cooper. "Come on now," he was saying. "Ain't worth it, Bud. Not this one." Buddy Cooper's eyes went big, and he seemed to realize what he was doing. The rest of the men followed Uncle Lucas's lead, telling Buddy Cooper to let the poor bastard go. Finally, he did. When released, the man crumpled to the ground, panting for breath. Under our feet, all of a sudden, the floor began to shake—this time in earnest—and the windows rattled in their panes. It was midnight, and I remembered the train. It blew past us, screeching. The shrill whistle sliced through Fay's, through all of us. Everyone watched Buddy Cooper, and Buddy Cooper watched the floor. No one toasted anything.

AUGUST: six months after my uncle died. The fair opened that night, and Aunt Mavis, for as long as I knew her, had never been one for the fair—"Too much bustle and fried food," she said—but I was a senior and would soon be leaving her for college. She claimed to be feeling nostalgic, so we went. An unexpected cold snap had settled over the Delta, so we wore our jackets, with the collars turned up high against the sharp wind. That night, we ate deep-fried Oreos and frosted funnel cakes. We rode the scrambler and the Ferris wheel and the tilt-a-whirl. We kept our heads spinning, our stomachs in a ceaseless churn. We tried, I think, to work ourselves into such a frenzy that we'd forget what we had lost earlier that year.

After touring the tornado-safety exhibit, we went to the coliseum. Inside, under the bright yellow lights, young girls in sparkling gowns and long gloves marched their pigs out into the center of the stadium amid the smell of the dirt floor and livestock. Entranced, we sat down in one of the first rows. Aunt Mavis rested her arm on the rusted railings and observed each one of the girls as she guided her pig up the stairs to the little podium and announced her name and her pig's name to the judges, as well as who her parents were, who was sponsoring her, and what she wanted to be when she was grown.

We stayed for the whole show. When they finally crowned that year's Little Miss Farm Special, Aunt Mavis cried. Her tears lasted until we got back to the car and started for home. During the drive back, she said, "You know, your uncle loved that pig as much as I did. Hell, he went with me that night to set it free."

After that, we were silent, keeping our eyes on the road. The defroster rattled, defogging the windows. The radio played a country song by an artist my mother had claimed to know. A great wealth of things existed between Aunt Mavis and me that we had decided, at some point or another, to leave unsaid—it had been our way—and having her talk now left me unsettled. I was no fool—of course, I'd always known something like this was the case, but actually hearing her reveal the truth behind one of my uncle's exaggerations felt like a betrayal of him and his memory. Like blasphemy. Still, I couldn't help myself.

I cut off the radio. "Go on."

"When we got there," she said, "it was too late, of course. The man had already hung Suzanne up by her hind legs. Cut her up something awful. My god, I never knew a pig could bleed so much."

THE BACHELOR PARTY, if that's even what it had been, ended with the last trills of the train whistle. The man with the mustache stumbled out the side door before anyone else, the first to disappear into the darkness. One by one, they all left, and when Buddy Cooper went to settle our tab, Uncle Lucas placed his arm around my neck, brought me close, and said, "How you feeling?"

I thought about this question for a long time. Then I said, "My teeth. My teeth are numb." Also, my head felt like someone had filled it with water, but I kept that to myself for some reason.

The girl frowned at me as I passed her going out the door. She said, "Come back and see me, little one."

"Yes, ma'am," I said, my face tingling. Buddy Cooper and my uncle roared with laughter as I slipped out the door ahead of them.

Once outside, Buddy Cooper told us his truck was close by. We should follow him, he said. My uncle clutched the back of Buddy Cooper's loose shirttail, and I held on to the back of my uncle's. We walked like this, in the dark, tethered to one another. Our feet made loud, slushy noises as we plodded through the debris of leaves and sticks. Trees crowded us on all sides, the color of bone. An animal moaned from its perch or nest behind us—a frog? A bird? I wasn't sure. I wondered, then, if I had died. Wildly, and perhaps drunkenly, I imagined I had croaked at the bar—my Culpepper heart finally giving out, going *kerplunk* for the last time—and this, then, was my afterlife: wandering around through the woods for time eternal. It was not an altogether unpleasant thought. I decided there must be worse fates. After all, I was here with my uncle. When we found Buddy Cooper's old blue Ford pickup, I almost suggested we camp there for the night, near the woods, shielded from the human world completely.

Buddy Cooper handed my uncle his keys. "You drive," he said. "I'm still too shaky from that bastard back there."

"Where we headed?" Uncle Lucas said.

"Sailor's choice. Anywhere, my friend, but here."

The inside of the truck smelled like chewing tobacco and motor oil. I sat squashed between them and watched bleary-eyed as the headlights blasted through the night, the lonely road opening up to receive us. I didn't know where we were headed until my uncle turned off onto Highway 51. He asked me when was the last time I'd been out to my parents' house in the country—the large farmhouse my mother could never sell or even rent.

As we pulled up the long driveway, the headlights caught most of the house in their beams. It seemed alien to me now, this large empty house, and with my buzz fading, I didn't have the heart to go in and longed, more than ever, to return to the safety of the trees.

We parked in the yard directly across from the front door so the headlights could shine into the house. Buddy Cooper said he didn't think this was such a good idea. "Hey, now," he was saying. "Let's us ease back over to my house. We can camp out there. Lois won't mind." Lois was the woman he would marry.

Uncle Lucas got out of the truck and walked to the front porch, then up the front steps.

My mother had given him a key to the place before she left. "Just in case," she had said, and I closed my eyes and pictured my mother's face, layered with makeup, her bleeding-red lips turned in a smile the last time I saw her, that day she left me with my aunt and uncle. My uncle unlocked the door to the house and walked inside. I hunched over my knees. I felt sick.

"You okay, kid?"

I sat back up and nodded.

"Sometimes," he said, "I think your uncle is like that doctor man, looking for the pieces of his heart even in places where he knows he won't find them."

"Do what?" Nothing made sense to me: the house, my uncle, what Buddy Cooper was saying. I felt like I had entered another person's life, stumbled into another story, one that refused embellishment but had to be told plainly and absolutely.

Buddy Cooper scratched my head and laughed. "You are Cooter Brown drunk." Then he slid out of the cab, and I followed him inside.

"Careful you don't fall," Uncle Lucas said to us.

The headlights illuminated the living room, revealing covered furniture, a broken clock on the wall, and duct-taped boxes scattered here and there on the floor. It was a ghost house, choked with the remnants of people I didn't know or care to know anymore even though I had once been one of them.

"Look,"Uncle Lucas said. "There's a couch for each of us."

"We're sleeping here tonight?" I said.

"You want us to go home to Aunt Mavis like this?"

Buddy shuffled from one foot to the other. "We can go back to my place. Drink some Crown and Cokes. It'll be fine."

Uncle Lucas waved this away. "Go if you want, Coop," he said. "We're camping here tonight."

"No, no. I can't leave y'all out here. I'll stay, I'll stay."

Once I got settled into one of the love seats, I didn't mind the house so much. Sleep came quickly, and I drifted off to the familiar sound of Uncle Lucas and Buddy Cooper whispering to each other. That night was my first alcohol-induced sleep, a cold sort of slumber I'd come to appreciate years later because, in the throes of it, I rarely dreamed.

When I awoke the next morning, I heard crying. The daylight came pounding through the shuttered windows, bright and horrible. I had to pee, badly, so I rolled off the love seat and ambled to the front porch, still half-dazed with sleep. On the porch swing, I found Uncle Lucas and Buddy Cooper in each other's arms. I said, "Hey, is it all right if I piss off the front porch?" But they didn't hear me at first because Buddy Cooper had his head back, sighing, and Uncle Lucas was kissing his neck.

Uncle Lucas slung himself off the swing. As if an invisible hand had snatched him by the scruff of his neck and thrown him. "Get back inside, goddamnit," he told me. He wiped his face and spit.

Frightened, I stumbled backward inside the house and perched awkwardly on one of the couch's armrests. They talked outside for about half an hour, whispering so I couldn't hear. I was embarrassed and felt like I had hurt them, offended my uncle, in seeing what I had seen. My head ached, and my bladder needed relief from all the gin and tonics the night before. Finally, I could take it no longer and went out back to relieve myself. When I returned, Uncle Lucas was leaning in the doorway, his eyes darting about the place, never settling on me or anything else. In the yard, Buddy Cooper's pickup rumbled to life.

My uncle said, "He'll call Mavis to come get us when he gets home."

"Sure," I said.

He kept standing. I sat down. We waited for nearly an hour without speaking. With great relief, we heard the crunch of gravel as Aunt Mavis's sedan pulled up the driveway. I stretched out in the back seat and pretended to fall asleep. Halfway home, Uncle Lucas rolled down his window and let the wind slap at his hair.

"You'll get the earache," Aunt Mavis said.

"Sick." He let back his seat and closed his eyes. "Carsick."

Aunt Mavis clicked her tongue. "Boys, boys," she said. "If you can't run with the big dogs, stay on the porch."

A WEEK LATER, Uncle Lucas moved out.

On the day of the move, he cleaned out his closet and chest of drawers and packed up everything he owned. I didn't know about it until it was too late to ask him to stay. Even if I had known earlier and tried to say something to him, I'm not sure that I would have. I was reading in my room when Aunt Mavis called me from downstairs to come say goodbye. She and I stood side by side, stock-still, as he paced in front of us saying that it would be better this way. More room for all of us. After he toted his last bag out to his truck, he came back and hugged Aunt Mavis. "I'll just be across town," he said. We could see him every day if we wanted. He shook my hand briskly. "You," he went to say but then stopped. He glanced back at Aunt Mavis and shook his head. "We are a strange sort, the three of us," he said, and with that, he left.

I'VE BEEN TRYING to tell the story of my uncle for some time now. He comes and goes in my thoughts perhaps more than anyone, even my mother. I always, finally, come back to that night at thc hospital morgue, his body recently delivered from Canada. Aunt Mavis had asked me to go with her. "Please," she had said, so I went.

A fat nurse led us to the cold room where they kept the bodies before the funeral home fetched them. My aunt clung to my arm as the nurse unceremoniously slid the body out from the metal lockers on one of those shiny slabs. Suddenly, there he was: Uncle Lucas.

"Can we have a minute?" Aunt Mavis said to the nurse. She nodded and told us she would come back in ten minutes or so after rounds. When she was gone, we inched closer to the body. "It's just us now," she said. "We are the last."

Then we heard a cough and jumped. Standing behind us was Buddy Cooper—a little fatter than when I last saw him but still wearing his tall cowboy hat. "I called him," Aunt Mavis explained to me.

Buddy Cooper couldn't meet my eyes as he stepped toward the table. His boots made loud *click-clack*s against the linoleum floor. He looked down at my uncle's body for the longest time.

"You better go on and touch him now," my aunt said. "Because he won't feel like himself when the funeral home gets through with him." So Buddy Cooper placed his hand on Uncle Lucas's smooth forehead. Like this, we quietly waited for the nurse to come back to us.

UNCLE LUCAS'S FUNERAL caused enough of a stir in our lives to bring home my mother from Nashville. According to her, things were good in Music City: She had landed a gig as the backup singer for Tanya Tucker and was slated to go on tour with her next month. "Soon," she told me, "we are going to be golden."

Seeing her for the first time in nearly eight years, I didn't know quite what to make of her, this woman, my mother: All that makeup made her look much older than I remembered, and her hair was dyed a frightening white blond and had been teased into great whorls above her head. "What are you?" I wanted to say to her. "What have you become?"

The only thing solid she knew about me was that I made good grades, that I hadn't made a B since the fifth grade—my aunt had dutifully mailed her copies of my report cards every nine weeks—so when people came up to us at the visitation service, she led off with this information. "My son here," she'd chime. "The scholar!" I really didn't know what to say to her; she asked me about college and I told her which ones I'd applied to. She asked about majors, and I listed off several that I thought would impress her. It soon became apparent to both of us that we spoke different languages, and trying to translate proved too painful.

For the graveside service, my mother had asked the Methodist preacher to say a few vague words about goodness and mercy. "Just in case," she said to Aunt Mavis. Besides the preacher and the workers at the funeral home, it was just the three of us huddled around the open mouth in the ground; I was standing between my aunt and my mother, each of them had an arm laced in mine. When the preacher finished, the workers slowly lowered the casket. Then something unexpected happened: My mother broke from us and began to sing, impromptu, "Love Lifted Me." Her voice fell off-key at times but was still beautiful and pure. My aunt and I looked up, following the delicate sounds as they floated up and up and over our heads.

WHEN I TELL THE STORY of my uncle, I want to end it there: my mother singing. It seems right to me. But I can't. Truth is, Buddy Cooper never showed up that night at the morgue, and my mother never sang in the cemetery. In fact, she never even made it to the cemetery; she went back to Nashville the night of the visitation. It was just Aunt Mavis and I: at the hospital, at the grave. In the real story, there was no repentant lover for dead Uncle Lucas and no song for me, only the hard silences left by the people we wanted—the people we craved the most—who had already moved on in their lives without us.

BREAK

We followed I-55 the whole way, a seemingly straight shot of blacktop cutting up northwest Mississippi—the part of the state that on maps resembles a protruding forehead. The first two hours were made up of hill after hill bleeding red clay and deep ditches soldiered by tall weeds. We had decided to take Forney's car, a dusty Honda Accord, and Regan sat beside him for the entire trip and sang with the radio, her eyes hidden by a large pair of sunglasses. She never offered to switch places with me even though the tiny back seat, filled with our luggage, had forced me to contort the great bulk of my body into the shape of a pretzel. I finally dozed off during the last half of the drive when the hills started to level out into fields complete with irrigation machines and faraway tractors and bulbous mounds of hay. When I woke up, my bad knee was throbbing, and there, outside my window, was Forney's Delta: flat, wide, mosquito heavy.

We arrived just after lunch, a sharp sun pressing down on us, the farmhouse shuttered and locked, flanked on either side by long stretches of gutted pasture. It was October, and Forney told me, as we pulled up the gravel driveway, that the farmers who rented the land from his mother had already started preparing the ground for freezing temperatures. A hard winter had been predicted in this year's *Farmers' Almanac*. It seemed ridiculous to me, the idea of winter, since fall hadn't even bothered to show up in the first place. Slick greens and summery yellows still shimmered in the pines and oaks. We had come here for the weekend to take a break from the thrumming outside world, to be secluded on all sides by a cathedral of trees.

While we were unloading the car, a large bearlike dog showed up at the edge of the yard. Silent and watchful, the dog seemed unsure of us, these strangers it'd caught trespassing. I like a dog to be a dog, to bark and huff and wag its tail, and this one's reluctance to do any of these sort of things unnerved me. All this is to say that I should have known the dog was trouble from the start.

"Old Hooch," Forney said. "The bastard lives."

Regan took off her sunglasses. "Is it mean?" she asked.

Forney laughed. "He's lived with my mother for most of his life. That would make anybody mean."

I was staying in Forney's old room upstairs while he and Regan were taking the master bedroom downstairs. After I put away my things and came back down, Forney and I decided to carry one of the couches in the living room outside. We picked the one that could easily seat three people and toted it through the narrow front door, angling the couch sideways to jimmy it on out. Meanwhile, Regan had disappeared into the kitchen to make us drinks.

"Let's test it out," Forney said, after we had shoved aside some expensive-looking metal rocking chairs and positioned the couch beside the porch swing. "I want to make sure I can sit here and see the sunrise in the morning." He glanced around him, at the feathering of bushes and shrubs that hid the highway, then at the great empty sky, as if he had never grown up here and was looking at these things for the first time. "This is east, right?" he said, pointing.

I plopped down beside him on the couch and nodded to my left. "More northeast, I think. Look at the angle of the sun above those pines."

He patted my knee. "You know such practical things, Tuck," he said. "That's why I'm a poet—I'm completely impractical."

While we were talking, Hooch plodded into the yard, its nose close to the ground, following a scent. The dog looked wild: fur mangy, leaves and cockleburs matted deep within the unwashed shag around its chest and rear legs. Forney began to explain the dog's sad history to me—how his mother had never penned or chained the dog when she first bought it, never bothered to train it either, letting the creature roam the uninterrupted acres of field and the small scratch of woods and riverbed behind the house. His mother had originally bought the dog for security purposes a few years after Forney's father died and she had some trouble getting rid of one of her boyfriends. Soon, though, she grew tired of it—much as she often did with her boyfriends. "Said she gave it to the woods," Forney was saying, his legs propped up on the porch railing. "But he always circles back here, like he's waiting for something. Maybe for someone. Poor son of a bitch."

Hearing this, I softened toward the animal and the way its ragged paws clutched at the ground as it slowly mulled about the yard. I got up from the couch and moved to the edge of the porch.

"Hooch," I called. "Here, boy."

The dog's floppy ears stiffened. It lifted its boxy head from a clump of monkey grass, meeting my eyes with its own dull black ones. We were just a few feet apart. "Here," I said again, and held out my hand, wiggling my fingers. "Come on, boy." The dog crooked its head sideways and began to trot my way like a pony. I noticed the flash of teeth just in time to pull back my hand, and the dog's jaws made a loud clapping noise as they clamped shut on empty air. I flew backward and landed awkwardly against one of the arms of the couch. Upset, the dog snorted, the first sound I'd heard it make since our arrival.

"Easy, boy," Forney said, and I wasn't sure if he was talking to me or the dog.

Regan, hearing me fall, had rushed outside. "My god," she said, speaking to Forney, breathless, "I was watching out the window, and for a minute, I thought I was gonna get to see them two go at it."

IT'S STILL A WONDER to me that I had become so close to Regan and Forney that first year of college. I'm usually best left to myself, partly because I had no brothers or sisters growing up in Vicksburg and enjoyed the silences that came with being an only child. Other people's voices, even my parents', usually made me itchy and nervous or want to hit something. This did not make me very popular in elementary school; it also didn't help matters much that I was a good foot taller than anyone else in my class. My bigness has always made me suspect. Only in high school, when I started playing football and sending quarterbacks to the emergency room, did I make a few friends. But even then, it was a friendship at a distance. Now I can't remember one of those boys I used to play with.

My senior year, I was a behemoth, having to duck or

turn sideways to enter most doorways. I had a way of filling up a room, crowding everyone and everything else out. By then, universities had started to take note of how adept I was at running down offensive lines, catching a player just below the rib cage with my helmet so hard and so fast that the impact would leave the player dazed and reeling. Scouts from Auburn and Tennessee and even LSU came to my big show. Oh, it was a heady time before I got hurt.

During a nonconference game, I made a run for a fumble and a thick bastard with a score to settle clipped me from behind. I fell funny and shattered my left kneecap. Doctor said it was like a metal vice smashing a walnut. In the three seconds it took for me to be brought down, I was done. Three surgeries later, my knee more metal than bone, the scholarships were all dried up, and the world seemed to clap shut almost as fast as it had opened. I realized soon enough that my story wasn't all that special: The washed-up athlete routine was a cliché even then, and no one, not even my high school coaches, was overly troubled. "Was in your cards, son," one said, when he came to see me in the hospital. Anyway, I don't want to talk about that. I want to focus on what happened *after*.

I ended up going to college anyway, picking the cheapest one I could find, a small regional school in central Mississippi, and majored in general business. College proved to be not quite the same as high school: People still made me nervous, but this time I didn't have football as a buffer. My bigness didn't work for me anymore either, and I began to sense that I was disappearing. Little by little, I felt myself dissolving like a cube of sugar in a mug of hot coffee. One day I'd walk out of my dorm room and no one would be able to see me. Naturally, this scared me. But what scared me more was that I looked forward to it, this vanishing. After all, there was a certain kind of peace that came with nothingness.

Then I became friends with Forney and Regan, and it all changed for me.

One night, I was in the bathroom, studying for a calculus test and feeling pretty raw about it. I'd made decent enough grades in high school, but I started to suspect that maybe the teachers had helped me along too much, for the sake of football, because I couldn't understand much of what the math textbook was trying to tell me to do. My roommate, a pale skinny kid who whined about how he missed his hometown and his friends, had turned out the lights and indicated that I needed to find someplace else to study. The library was closed at that hour, and the study hall on our floor usually had too many people in it for me to concentrate, so the bathroom seemed like my best bet.

Our dormitory was set up to where every two rooms shared a bathroom between them. After about ten minutes of reading about limits and derivatives in the bathroom that connected my room to Forney's, I started hearing these muffled cries coming from Forney's door. It took me a minute to realize that the sounds were those of a girl. The college was very strict about decency and morals, and girls were forbidden from entering a male dormitory. I set my textbook down and listened, not believing that the hawkish-looking boy I lived next door to had a woman in his room and marveling at his ability to smuggle her in. That took talent. After a while, I began to differentiate more subtle noises coming from the room: the plastic squeak of the twin mattress, the fast, wet thump of his body against hers, the wistful voice of the girl calling out his name—his strange name, *Forney! Forney!*—over and over. I almost laughed. I might have if the whole thing didn't make me so desperately sad. Here I was, a former all-state defensive tackle, reduced to listening to other people's lovemaking. What I did next was perhaps most shameful of all: I got up from the toilet. I placed my ear to the door and tried to imagine what the girl looked like. I wondered if she was pretty and hoped she wasn't.

The sounds kept going on for some time, getting louder, until someone started banging on the hallway door.

"Open on up," the voice said. It was our resident assistant, a pimply prelaw student who took his job seriously. The dorm room went silent, and I leaned in closer to the door, spreading my hands along the frame to balance myself. There was a shuffle of footsteps, some whispers.

"Who is it?" asked Forney. He was buying time, I knew that much. Some kind of plan was forming in there.

"You know who, Forney. Open up."

When it was too late, I realized that the couple was heading for the door I stood behind. The door opened slowly; they were careful not to make the usual loud clicking noise. Forney shoved the girl inside and shut the door behind her, leaving her alone, wide-eyed and completely naked, staring at me as if I were the one who had intruded on her. I looked away from her body. First at the toilet, which seemed somehow to be more insulting than getting an eyeful, so I moved my eyes to the sink counter instead, focusing on the sight of my textbook.

I held my hands up, and said, "Just leaving, ma'am," but the girl shushed me. When I looked at her face, she had put a finger to her lips. A loud conversation was going on behind her through the door. "All your money can't buy you special privileges, Culpepper," the resident assistant was saying. "Not here. Not on my floor." The naked girl and I stood there no more than a few feet apart. I stopped fighting my instinct to be gentlemanly and discreet. Gave into the urge to look at her, to gaze at the way her bare shoulders, the color of warm light, curved into arms; at her round breasts, each kissed with a brown nipple; and farther down, below her waist, at the tuft of hair between her legs, still oozy and gleaming from the sex I'd heard her having. She was the first girl I had ever seen completely in the nude outside of the dirty movie I'd stolen from under one of my cousins' beds and the *Hustlers* I'd found in junior high in the toolbox of an abandoned truck by the river. The girls I'd gone to bed with in high school had kept most of their clothes on, as did I. Sex with them had been like a more advanced form of shaking hands, polite and firm but still impersonal.

The girl watched me watching her. She smiled and curtseyed dramatically. I started to say something when I remembered the trouble they were in. The penalty for having a girl in your room was suspension for a whole semester. The resident assistant was not giving up either. He would soon, after checking under the bed and in the midsize day closet, come for the bathroom, the next obvious place to stash someone in a hurry. In a moment of inspiration, I gestured to the sink, to the box-shaped cabinet below it. The girl nodded, understanding me immediately. She opened the cabinet door and stooped to enter it after blowing me a thank-you kiss. I was charmed.

The resident assistant barged into the bathroom a few minutes too late and found me sitting on the sink, my face crammed into my textbook, my large legs dangling over the cabinet door. He looked truly puzzled. Forney, however, when he followed the resident assistant into the bathroom, appeared thunderstruck. “Hey,” I said, making my voice sound strained and annoyed.

“Did you see a girl come in here?” asked the RA.

“A girl?” I can play dumb really well when I want to.

Frustrated, the resident assistant turned to Forney, who was shrugging. It was obvious that he had no idea what I was doing there either. If the resident assistant had pressed further, he would have noticed how my hands were trembling as I held the textbook and that my ears were bright red. But my presence had caught him off guard, made him sloppy. He could only shake his head, and he finally ambled out of the bathroom, mumbling something as he left, declaring defeat before I'd have thought he would have. After he was gone, Forney and I waited a couple of minutes before we made our next move, each of us taking the other in. I'd seen him only once before, from across our dorm hall on move-in day. I didn't think much about him at the time except how jealous I was that he could afford a private room. Now I saw him more closely: He had dark purple circles under his eyes and the lean frame of a running back. Muscular but not bulky like me. When I thought it was safe, I jumped down from the countertop and helped the girl unwind herself from the tiny enclosure under the sink. When upright, she winked at Forney, who now smirked, and then she leaned in close to my neck to kiss me on the cheek. Her lips felt like a damp rag against my face, the kind I would use to wash the grease off from under my eyes after games. "Good thinking, man," Forney said, and for a moment, both of them smiled.

"Just look at him," the girl said.

"A fucking grizzly."

There was a familiar tone in their voices; something I hadn't heard since getting to college: the sound of awe. It went through me like a heavy wave—the whole Gulf of Mexico was in their voices, bathing me. Then they were gone. I stayed in the bathroom for the rest of the night even though I'd given up studying. I killed the lights and sat on the cool bathroom floor. Forney's dorm room remained silent, almost as if the two people, once in there, had ceased to exist altogether.

AFTER THAT NIGHT in the dorm, I began seeing them around campus more and more. Always in my periphery: in the cafeteria two tables over, in the magazine room at the library, outside on the drill field. Each time, Forney had a book in his hand and wore a serious, strained look on his face as if he were constipated. Most of the time, she was with him, her arm sometimes slung around him in some way or another. She usually wore a long skirt—the kind you see girls from California wearing—and chunky bracelets and rings. Her blue eyes, the most startling thing about her, were usually shielded by aviator sunglasses or thickly coated with eyeliner. The two of them looked like they belonged on an album cover. I think now that maybe they were following me, that we were scoping one another out. We would nod when I passed them, and soon, we started speaking, and then, before I knew it, we were having full-throated conversations.

From the start, they were a mystery. There are still things about them I don't know, like how they met, how long they'd been together before I came along. Forney told me once during one of our impromptu talks that he thought of himself as something of a poet, although he'd never written any poems to date. Instead, he spent his mornings retyping the work of other poets—Ginsberg, Stevens—on a sky-blue IBM Correcting Selectric II, the tapping and clanging of that machine so loud at times that I could hear him going at it through the cinder-block walls in my dorm room. His whole poetry thing, all that typing, was something I didn't get. When I asked him about it, he said, "I've not found the right words for me yet, so I'm using other people's until then." He had a moony way of talking that could make you think he was pretentious, and I didn't like him very much at first, not as much as I liked Regan anyway. He surprised me, though, when he got into an argument with my roommate.

My roommate, Arnold, had a habit of using the hair dryer in the mornings, its loud, hoarse yawl sometimes waking me up when the kid had an eight o'clock class. It ticked me off a little. But it drove Forney crazy. One morning, still half-asleep, I heard them in the bathroom arguing. "Fucking messing up my flow," Forney was saying to him when I made it to the doorway. "I need quiet in the morning, dude." He was holding my roommate's Ionic Turbo Styler and wearing nothing but a pair of flannel pajamas. When he saw me, he smiled as if he had been expecting me. "You know what I'm talking about, don't you, Tucker," he said. "A man can't think with all this racket. His precious hair can towel dry."

My roommate—now I feel a little sorry for him; he must have been terrified—glanced at me in a way that told me he thought I could save him.

"He's sorry," I told Forney.

"Wasteful," Forney said. "Look at the lights." Forney plugged the hair dryer into the outlet above the sink, and the bulbs dimmed. "See?"

"I think," Arnold began, then stopped. Forney had just yanked the hair dryer from the outlet and cracked it in half with his hands as if it were a wishbone. "You broke my hair dryer," my roommate said. Forney let the pieces fall out of his hand, and they clacked against the tile floor. Arnold turned to me: "He broke my hair dryer."

"For your own good," Forney said, taking the tone of a

parent. He had impressed me. I didn't think the wannabe poet had it in him.

"Tell him, Tucker," he said. "Tell him what I mean."

But Arnold didn't wait for me to say anything. He picked up the broken pieces, held the handle in one hand, the shattered heat cone in the other. "My fucking hair dryer," he said. "You're crazy." He looked at Forney, then at me. "The both of you. Completely nuts." He stormed out of the bathroom just as Forney and I began to cackle.

Over the years, there have been a lot of things that I've forgotten—the name of my first grade teacher, my mother's favorite color—but these memories with Forney still spark with clarity, especially this one, and I think it's because in that moment in the bathroom, both of us laughing at that poor boy, we became friends, not just people who spoke to each other.

Later in the evening, we went out drinking. Forney, a fifth-year senior, was over twenty-one and had no trouble procuring us a fat bottle of Wild Turkey. We drove his Honda into a nearby field of buckshot and got soused. Between us, we finished the bottle, and we started singing David Allan Coe and Conway Twitty songs, harmonizing to a network of stars, blinking and uncaring. The night wore on, and he eventually had to call Regan to come pick us up. "Save us from ourselves," he yelled into the pay phone of the truck stop we'd walked to. I had to help Forney into the back seat when Regan got there; he was far worse off than I was. On the drive back, he started singing the chorus of "You've Never Been This Far Before," and Regan placed her hand on the crotch of my blue jeans.

"You were listening, weren't you?" she said, her voice slicing through Forney's dissonant singing. "That night before I came in. You were listening to us fucking. It's okay."

When I didn't answer right away, she squeezed. "You are trouble, girl," I said, and stared at her hand as it began to rub me through my jeans. She touched me without tenderness, her boyfriend not more than a foot behind us in the back seat, which made the whole experience more exciting. We didn't go any further than that, her touching, and Forney never noticed a thing.

FOR THE NEXT FEW WEEKS, the three of us spent much of our free time together. We would ride around town listening to Regan's CDs—she forbid us to play country music in her presence—and we usually ended the night with Forney and me sitting on the hood of his car watching her dance to Liz Phair's "Never Said": "*All I know is I'm clean as a whistle, baby,*" she sang to us, her voice husky. We went to a lot of movies, and most of the time, I sat between them in the dark theater, our breathing taking the same pattern after a while. We saw *Jurassic Park* twice at the dollar theater, and I can still remember Forney's astonishment when the computer-generated brachiosaur filled up the giant screen. "Amazing," he whispered. "Just amazing." When I was with them in moments like these, I thought that this—this closeness? This friendship?—is what keeps a body from disappearing, from dissolving away. And I started to wonder if I had been so drunk that I'd imagined Regan's hand on me—she never acknowledged that it'd happened even in the rare moments we were alone.

One morning we were sitting outside on the grass near the large sundial by the student union, and they asked me to go away with them for the weekend. "You should come," Forney said. "Mother has gone to Barbados. One of her extended cruises."

"The house is supposed to be huge," Regan said. "We can play hide-and-go-seek for hours."

"In the middle of nowhere for three days," I said. "Tempting."

Regan threw a pinecone at me. "He's coming."

Forney said, "He seems determined."

"Oh, he's coming," she told Forney, and I felt as if I were some kind of wild animal they were talking about, an animal they thought couldn't understand them. "It's fall break," she said, "and he hasn't got anywhere else to go."

I KEPT AN EYE on Hooch while we lounged on the front porch, drinking tall glasses of gin and tonic. The more I drank, the more comical the dog became. After the near bite, it retreated to the spidery shadow of a sweet gum, where it stayed for the rest of the afternoon. By evening, with the sky coated in fiery oranges and reds, Regan and I had moved from the porch to the side of the house so we could soak up the last bits of the afternoon light and give Forney some space—he'd brought his electric typewriter with him and was itching to use it. You could always tell when he was ready to write: His eyes would glaze over and he'd chew on the tips of his fingers. He'd get all nervous. I had often wondered just what went on inside his brain that kept him from writing his own poetry and always figured it must have been something like a jumble of words, all twirling and switching around in there, an endless combination that was maddening for him. I think the poems he retyped settled him, gave order to the chaos in his brain.

While he typed, Regan and I ventured to the tin shed and found, amid the rusty Bush Hog and menacing-looking combine and other pieces of bladed farm equipment I don't have words for, an old hammock, yellowed but still functional. We carried it outside and fastened it between two sturdy-looking pines.

The dog shuffled out of the shade and came to investigate. When it got close, sniffing and slobbering, I lost my balance for a minute and stumbled against the hammock, almost falling in it.

"You are drunk," Regan said. "Drunk, drunk, drunk." She shook her head when she spoke, letting her buttery yellow hair fall over her face.

"Not so much," I said, and the dog sat down a few feet from us, placing its head on top of its massive paws. I tapped the hammock, making the net swing casually as if moved by the breeze. "Ready for the lazy and the free," I said, which I thought was witty. Reagan frowned.

"I need more gin." She was wearing a purple bikini top, and the rhinestone in her belly button was glittering like a fleck of shattered glass. She wobbled a little as she tried to maneuver herself in the hammock, which made me realize she was a little drunk too. Once settled, she undid her top. "Heaven," she said quietly, and I had the impression that she had forgotten I was there, but then she held her hand out to me, and said, "We need some vitamin D. Come lie with me and be my friend."

I slid to the ground faster than I had intended and became dizzy. The gin was really working on me now that I had slowed down to let it. My head was beginning to feel too heavy for my neck, and I imagined it breaking off and rolling across the yard, the dog playfully chasing behind it. "Don't think Hooch will ever cotton to us," I said.

Regan lifted her head and considered the dog. "It's so ugly, but then again there must be something special about a dog that's all bite and no bark."

"Maybe it's forgotten how—to bark, I mean." I rubbed my tongue along my teeth; my mouth was dry, and my molars felt as if they didn't belong in there. "I need another drink."

"Ooh, me too, me too."

I got back to my feet rather easily, but it took me a second or two to remember why I'd gotten up in the first place. Before I could leave, Regan's hand caught the elastic band of my gym shorts and pulled me over to her. Her fingers traced my thigh before disappearing up my shorts. Her hand felt good, just as it had that night in the car, and I let her touch me for a moment. If I had been soberer, I might have gotten angry with the way she randomly put her hands on me, as if I were hers. I wasn't angry, but I grabbed her on the wrist, and that was enough for her to stop and take her hand away. "He can probably see you," I said, and she pulled down her sunglasses to the crook of her nose. Her eyes were pure and absolute, no eyeliner on them.

"Scaredy-cat," she said. "Be quick with the drink. I want to go to bed good and stupid."

Forney barely noticed me as I passed him on the porch. He had added an old desk to the furniture outside and was sitting there with his typewriter. A thin paperback was propped up on a chair in front of him. He was hunched over the machine comparing what he had written to what was on the page.

Inside the kitchen, I took two quick shots of tequila and then made the drinks, being generous with the gin and the ice. As I walked back outside, the breezeway shifted under my feet, as if I were in a fun house. I stumbled a bit, falling against the wall, knocking down a picture of some man in his army greens who looked like Forney only ten years older. It had to be his father. He had the same serious eyes, the same hard mouth. I sat the drinks down on a coffee table and picked up the framed photo. His daddy came from money. Probably didn't know anything about trailer parks and would shudder at the thought of someone like me staggering, half-drunk, in his house. "Old fucker," I said aloud, and hung it back on the wall. Only then did I see a crack in the glass; it ran diagonally across the picture. My stomach began to clench, and I doubled over, almost throwing up right there on the shag carpet.

"Fuck," I said, rising, speaking to the man in the picture. "I *am* drunk."

Forney met me at the doorway. Took the drinks. "Let me," he said. "You look like you've had too much sun. Stay here and cool off, buddy."

I leaned my head against the porch railing and watched

him go to her, speculating on if she'd touch him as she had touched me. I thought I should be jealous, but I couldn't quite summon the emotion. I liked them together, and I liked how I revolved around them like a satellite. She didn't belong to me, but I belonged to them.

I sat down in front of Forney's typewriter. He had run an extension cord from the living room to power it and had forgotten to turn it off. The machine was still humming, ready for fingers. The poem being retyped was called "Silence." It was short, so I was able to read the whole thing. And the last lines had a way of sticking to me even though I was drunk.

Nor was he insincere in saying,
"Make my house your inn."
Inns are not residences.

I said the last lines to myself. Not satisfied, I said them again, only louder. I said them to the world. Then I heard Regan squeal and remembered Hooch, that awful mangy dog. I imagined the creature's slobbery jaws tearing into Regan, mangling her soft skin. I stumbled off the front porch toward the hammock, a wave of nausea passing over me. I knew it wouldn't be long now before I threw up. When I reached them, I saw Forney first. He stood with his arms crossed, frowning.

"What?" I said. He nodded toward Regan. She was

crouched down by the hammock, laughing as the dog licked an ice cube out of her hand with its thick red tongue.

"I think he likes the taste of gin," she said to us.

"Wrong." Forney shook his head. "Think he likes the taste of you."

I sunk to the ground and finally wretched.

EVENING SETTLED AROUND the house, and the dimming sky was a comfort. My temples were still tender and aching from when I threw up, and relaxing in the Jacuzzi on the deck didn't help much. I had been in a whirlpool many times in high school, usually at the end of a week of two-a-days, but I had always been alone. It was different having two other people in there with me. Made me more cautious of my movements, careful not to touch a stray foot with my own. We had been in there for about half an hour, not speaking, the steam from the hot water creating a kind of fog around us, when Regan got out and told us that she needed to cool off some.

Alone, the two of us sat there facing each other, no sound except the air jets. The lights in the floor of the Jacuzzi didn't work anymore. The sky had purpled into night, and we found ourselves in darkness, pure and complete. "Sex," Forney said suddenly, "is supposed to be safest in here. The hot water kills the sperm."

I lifted my head from the lip of the Jacuzzi and saw nothing: black shapes over a darker black. "Sex is never safe. Not really," I said, and it was like speaking inside a cave. It was as if my voice were not my voice but his voice echoing back to him from a curved wall of stone. We could hear Regan calling the dog, and I imagined the large creature running toward her, tongue hanging out.

"Regan can get anything to love her. When she wants to," Forney said.

The mosquitoes were beginning to nip at my ears, so I sank deeper in the water, going completely under for a while.

"Tell me," Forney was saying when I came back up. "What's the most embarrassing thing you've ever done?" I shook the water out of my ears and acted as though I hadn't heard the question. He didn't wait long for me to answer before he started speaking, his voice dropping an octave. "After Daddy died, Mother installed this Jacuzzi. Started bringing her boyfriends. Once I watched her fuck a man in here. I was in my room, at my window. Didn't think they could see me from up there. Later that night, he came to my bedroom and shook me awake. Don't know what kept me from pissing myself. He said he saw me watching. Called me a pervert and told me that if I ever spied on them again he'd pluck my eyes out with a spoon."

"Jesus," I said, not wanting to hear any more.

The light fixture beside the Jacuzzi flickered on, and I covered my eyes. "That light never cuts on at the right time. Sensors are broken. Goddamn."

Forney paddled to the side of the tub where I was and reached behind me to the light switch. In a flash, we were in darkness again.

"What about you?" Forney asked.

I thought back to my childhood in Vicksburg: my parents, those dented and rusted trailers that made up my neighborhood, the river sludge that would sometimes wash right up to our wooden steps, the smoky casino boats, my years playing football, my injury, and having to quit and leave that part of myself behind—it all seemed so insignificant now, almost as if it had happened to another person. I imagined my mind was a chest of drawers and began to open each of them, searching for something, cleaning out the hurt and the disappointment.

"Horses," I said to him. He jumped in the water as if he'd fallen asleep and my voice had woken him. "I don't like riding them. The few times I've ridden, I always let the horse go where it wants to. We usually end up lost."

"They scare you?"

"No, not that. I just don't like the feeling of controlling another living thing like that. Having this great big animal under you, forcing it to go your way when all it probably wants to do is eat grass and rut in ditches." I'd never said this—or even knew I thought it—until that moment. "Maybe that's why your mama let Hooch go."

"Pretty to think so," he said. His voice had changed again; it was thin and hurt me to hear it. I dipped the back of my head in the water and gazed up at the sky.

LATER THAT NIGHT, in Forney's old room, I couldn't sleep. Instead, I fingered through all of his books that lay scattered across the floor and on the desk beside the window. Books by people I'd never heard of before. They frustrated me for some reason, much like the picture of his father had. The feeling, however, didn't last long. I remembered Forney out there in the Jacuzzi, festering like an open wound, and it evaporated. I leaned over the desk and looked out the same window he had as a boy when he'd spied on his mother. The Jacuzzi was turned off and covered. The light beside it had been turned back on, and I could see beyond the deck out into the backyard, where the dog was lying. "You," I said, and the dog unburied its head from its paws and looked up as if it had heard my voice. I stepped back from the window, startled. I gave it a minute and looked again. The dog was still staring up in my direction.

The next morning, Forney wanted to ride four-wheelers on the dirt paths behind the house and didn't want the dog lurking behind us, so he suggested that we put him in the old chicken pen by the shed. I didn't think the three of us had enough muscle to move the dog anywhere it didn't want to go. Forney was confident, though, and assured us that he could handle it. He placed a slice of raw meat—a dark gray mystery meat that he'd found in the freezer—in the center of the pen, and we waited for the dog to take the bait, but it stayed clear.

Frustrated, Forney approached the dog with a leash, with the intention of dragging it into the pen. The closer he got to the dog, the more it started to growl, and I thought I was about to hear it bark. The dog snapped at him, and Forney kicked the ground, cussing, which seemed to agitate the dog even more.

"Maybe," I told him, "we should lay off and go if we are going."

"No," Forney said. "I'm tired of pussyfooting around Hooch. Got to learn it's a dog. Goddamn." He had been on edge all morning, not even taking time to type. I chalked it up to being hung over. God knows, I didn't feel my best.

"What's going on out here?" Regan had come back outside, her hair damp from the shower. The dog stopped growling the moment it saw her. She patted her leg, and the dog went to her. As she scratched its ears, the dog whimpered. "It's only angry because it's so dirty. Aren't you, boy?" She told us to go on ahead without her, that she was tired of looking at this animal and wanted to clean it up.

Forney threw up his hands and started walking off to the shed where the two Yamaha Grizzlies were kept. Her interest in the dog was beginning to worry me some. I waited until he was out of earshot.

"The fuck you doing?" I asked her. But she gave no indication that she had heard me. She turned and headed back to the house, the dog following close behind.

Before leaving, Forney pulled out a dirty cap from a toolbox and shoved it on my head. "For the sun," he said, and then we were off. I enjoyed driving the four-wheeler down the dirt paths, following Forney on his. We zigzagged through the thick of the woods and came out beside a nearby field. I was able to put Regan out of my mind when I had to worry about the rough trail and keeping my wheels in the same tracks as Forney's so I didn't flip. We eventually ended up at a little river, and we parked our ATVs on a little sandbar, side by side, just inches from the water. He had brought two cane poles and a tackle box full of gummy lures, and we fished the dark water until the sun started to droop behind the trees. Having no luck, we decided to give it up and go home.

Before cranking up the four-wheelers, Forney said, "Regan's gonna leave me soon."

This was the first time he'd ever talked about their relationship to me. Felt as if I were eavesdropping. I told him that we were all tired and had drunk too much the night before.

"No," he said. "I feel it in her body when she lies next to me. Has a way of freezing you out when she wants to."

"For fuck's sake," I said, and turned the key to my Grizzly. The engine roared to life. "You don't know what you don't know."

"AND WHAT BOUNTY did my men bring me?" Regan said to us when we pulled up. She lay on the porch couch. Her hair was tousled, and she wore a fluffy cotton bathrobe. "Ah," she said as we neared. "They came back with empty hands. What are we going to do with them?" When we made it to the steps, the dog stood and began to growl, a low throaty rumble. Like falling gravel. "Shh," she said, and touched the dog's back. It had been cleaned; its fur, while still dingy, had been combed and was fluffy; all the debris had been washed away.

"See you've been busy," I said.

"Hooch, is that you?" Forney was blinking slowly. "He looks—"

"Isn't he precious," Regan said. The dog was weary of us and backed up against Regan's knees. Forney sighed and went inside. But I lingered behind.

"What's his problem?" asked Regan.

I wanted to tell her what he'd told me, ask her if it was true. Ask her if she was leaving him. Ultimately, I shrugged.

The sky was clear tonight, and a few stars were starting to blink on, looking fragile and pink, hanging so close that I felt as if I could thump them away if I wanted.

I showered downstairs. The water pressure was much stronger than it had been upstairs, and when I finished, my skin felt clean and new. I put on a pair of dorm pants and a gray T-shirt, the last of my clean clothes. When I joined the other two in the living room, they were quiet and not looking at each other. Both of them seemed genuinely relieved to have me there. I felt like a child who had walked in on his parents arguing and wished, suddenly, that we were leaving tonight, not the following morning. Something was slipping away from us, and I thought at the time that if we left then we might have a chance to go back to the way we were before we left.

Regan smiled. "Feel better?"

"Spick-and-span," I said, trying to lighten the mood, but the silence persisted.

Forney cooked burger patties in the oven, baking them in tinfoil with onions and butter. We ate them without buns on paper plates. Regan had made a crunchy salad with diced pecans and toasted ramen noodles and a sweet vinaigrette. The mismatched meal was good. I didn't realize how hungry I had become. The quiet was broken when Regan said, coyly, "This would have been better with fish." Forney let her words disappear into the air without comment.

"Let's be nice," I said.

"Forney," Regan said. She threw her fork at him, and he dodged it. "You, Forney."

I gathered the plates and took them to the trash in the kitchen. I wanted them to fix things while I was gone; I wanted to go back in the room and find them all right again. As I was placing the forks in the sink, Regan's thin arms slipped around my waist. She had snuck into the kitchen without my hearing her. "Cut it out." I shoved her away and went to the refrigerator. I kept my back to her. Her touch made me crazy, made my thoughts turn gooey and unformed. I put the rest of salad into the icebox, and when I turned around, she was grinning in such a way that made me, all two hundred and something pounds of me, afraid of her.

"What are you doing?" I realized what a fierce creature she was. Saw the fierceness prickling off her skin. She put her hand behind my neck and pulled me to her. And then we were kissing. Her mouth was warm and soft, and I lost myself to the feel of it. Behind her, I saw Forney standing in the doorway. Maybe he had been there all along. I don't know. I pushed her off of me, and she fell away, laughing, wiping her lips.

"Don't this make a pretty picture," he said. Regan stretched out her arm toward him, and he went to her, as if she were some kind of goddess that he'd come to pay tribute to. She kissed him just as she had kissed me, and I went hard. I felt drugged, drunk again, as if my kneecaps had been replaced by balloons. Arm in arm, they moved closer to me, as if this were the most natural thing in the world. My chest tightened when she grabbed my shirt and brought me to them. The three of us stood in the kitchen in a kind of awkward dance. Regan leaned her head on Forney's shoulder and sighed, becoming soft. It was easy then, or maybe it just seemed easy, being with them like this. Something that was started months ago, the night we first met in the dorm, had finally opened up and lay exposed. There was nothing to be done but to follow through with what we were doing.

Regan led us to the master bedroom, and sometime later in the night, my body still wrapped in theirs, I thought I heard barking.

I WOKE UP ALONE, my legs tangled in the sheets. The glint of the sun told me it was late, possibly the afternoon. The mattress sat crookedly on the bed frame, and the square room, his mother's room, shimmered with gold wallpaper. Like waking up in a jewelry box. I could hear Forney on the front porch, pecking away on the typewriter at a furious pace. When I leaned up to look out the window, I saw Regan playing with Hooch. She had found a Frisbee and was tossing it into the air, and the dog, a dutiful playmate, lumbered after it each time.

I put on my shirt and boxers, and ambled into the kitchen, scratching my head. I went to the sink and turned on the faucet. Splashed my face with the cold well water and patted it dry with a paper towel. When I stepped outside, Forney stopped typing and turned.

"How you feel?" he said. There was a slight quiver in his voice. So much depended on what I said next. I knew it; he knew it.

"I feel," I said, choosing my words carefully. "I feel very European." Both of us howled with laughter. I stepped out into the sunlight, felt invigorated. There wasn't a book propped up in front of his typewriter; he was either writing a poem from memory or this was something original.

Forney smiled, seeing me realize this. "It started this morning. New stuff. My stuff."

I leaned in to read what he had written, but he covered the page with his hand. "No, no," he said. "Not ready yet, sport." He slapped a stack of papers beside him. "Been through some drafts this morning but still rusty as hell."

"This is great."

"Listen, I think Regan's back. I mean, whatever happened last night, it worked. It helped us. All of us. We're better now. Right?"

I told him the world felt right to me. I leaped off the porch in my bare feet, and Regan never saw me coming. I swiped the Frisbee from her hand, throwing it hard into the horizon. The dog, ears cocked, was unable to resist and took after the disk not long after it left my hand.

"Well," she said. "Someone slept well."

"Wish we could stay like this forever—just the three of us, away from everybody."

She put her hands in her pockets and stepped away from me, as if we were strangers. "We leave today."

I smiled. "There will be more breaks."

She clicked her tongue like an offended librarian. "About that. I think Forney and I need to be alone for a while when we get back. Work on us, you know."

"Yeah, right."

I closed the space between us in one step and picked her up by the hips, spinning her in the air. "Put me down," she said, and she began to hit my shoulders. "Put me down right now." But I didn't want to hear what she was saying and pressed her body close to mine, wanting to feel what I felt the night before. She had changed. I stopped spinning and looked up into her face. Thought I could find some trace of the woman who was there the night before.

"What about—?" I said, and she started to laugh.

Her nails scraped along my neck. "What? You think

because we suck your dick," she said, laughing a little more, "that we want you around all the time?"

I let her go, and she tumbled to the ground, landing on her elbows. She threw a clod of dirt at me. I kicked it away and was too late in seeing the dog coming toward me, as quick as a panther. Hooch had me pinned beneath him, his claws piercing my chest, before I could react. The breath was knocked out of me, and I had just enough time to brace the dog around the neck with my arms to keep its snapping mouth from mangling my face.

"Call him off," I said to Regan, but she backed away from us, her face pinched and uncertain. My arms were getting tired, and Hooch, impatient, was becoming more and more vicious. I almost felt sorry for the dog, for what we had done to it, intruding into its territory. After all, the dog was trembling with the same love I had felt; like me, it was trying desperately to protect the few specks of happiness it had probably ever felt in its whole miserable life. My arms gave out, and I shut my eyes, waiting for it to make ground chuck out of my face and neck. I hoped it would be fast. The dog, however, was stopped. Forney had snatched it from behind, and when I opened my eyes, he had the frenzied animal in a headlock, its paws slashing at air. In one quick movement, before I knew what was happening, Forney twisted the dog's head all the way back. There was a sharp snap. The dog's paws went limp. Forney didn't seem to realize what he had done at first, and when he did, he let out a long cry.

When Regan touched his arm, he jumped. "Let it go," she said. He looked relieved to have someone to tell him what to do and, all at once, dropped the dog. Hooch fell beside me, a pile of fur and teeth and claws.

Forney rushed inside the house, and Regan and I gazed at the dog, then at each other. Neither of us knew what to say, I think. When Forney came back, he was carrying a tarp. Without speaking, Forney and Regan wrapped up the dog and carried him to the back of one of the four-wheelers we had left parked in the front yard yesterday. I followed them and was about to get on the other four-wheeler, but Forney, seeing where I was headed, stepped in my way and pushed me back with both hands, almost knocking me back to the ground.

"You coming?" he said, and he was speaking to Regan, who nodded and got on the four-wheeler. "Hold on to him, okay?" She put an arm behind her, around the large mass they'd hooked onto the back grille. The four-wheeler roared to life. I didn't watch them leave. I walked back to the porch and saw that the typewriter was empty. I didn't have the heart to look in the trash. I went on inside to pack my clothes, but I didn't have enough energy to gather them up, so I went back outside and sat on the porch couch, and in the distance, the sound of the four-wheeler went abruptly silent, which meant they'd found a spot to bury the dog. They would be quick. It was getting dark, and we still had the long drive back to our old lives.

LADY TIGERS

Rusty sat behind the wheel of the bus and watched the sky turn sour. A year ago, when his father had coached the Lady Tigers, he'd been expected to serve as the team's water boy in addition to his regular duties as their bus driver. But Coach Culpepper, bless him, had no such expectations. He told Rusty he could stay on board. After all, Rusty was a senior and probably had important tests to study for. He didn't.

Last night, after her shift at the Piggly Wiggly, his mom had brought him home the latest *Catwoman* to help him pass the time during the ball game, but his attention had been sidetracked by the onslaught of sky bracketed within the bus's windshield. Skies were bigger in the Delta than in the hilly country he was used to. He knew that—everyone did—and yet its bigness still surprised him. The sky pushed on and on. Great swaths of blue every which way. It was a marvel the Lady Tigers could hobble bases and throw balls with so much vastness bearing down on them. Eventually, he spotted in the distance a blue so deep it was purple. Only not purple, no. A sootiness inching toward the ballpark. An infection.

For two innings, the thundercloud spread, billowing out of itself like smoke, soaking up light as it grew. The bus didn't face the diamond, but Rusty could make out the sounds of the game, the clink of metal bats, the random chants from the opposing team, the Lady Stars. *Now hush, you don't want none of us!* Before he realized it, late morning looked more like early evening, and a vein of lightning cracked through the cloud mass. Fat raindrops followed, slapping hard against the windshield, warping the world liquid.

Then he heard them: the Lady Tigers, as they slammed against the side of the bus like blind cows, hollering to be let inside. He pulled the lever above the stick, and the accordion-like door squeezed open. In they hurtled, one by one, smelling of sweat and hair spray, popping Bubble Yum, clad in their black and gold uniforms. Number 12 lumbered up first. Eyeblack smeared down her rosy cheeks, her topknot all but destroyed. The bat bag strapped to her shoulders nearly clocked him in the side of the head as she plodded by. More of them were close behind, pushing to get in out of the rain: Numbers 45 and 62 and 33 and 8. They were yammering on about a female ref's bad calls and possible "dykeyness." "Licky, Licky," said Number 16, the only black Lady Tiger, causing her teammates to squeal.

By the time the coach shoved on, he was soaked. His black polo clung to his torso, his nipples poking through. He held a clipboard in one hand and toted an orange Gatorade cooler with the other.

"Naw, your poor coach don't need any help," he said, fake mad and huffing.

The Lady Tigers tittered.

"You'll melt in the water, Coachie," Number 36 said. "You so sweet."

Rusty tried to grab the cooler, but the coach waved him away with his clipboard, dousing Rusty's glasses with rainwater.

"Crank us up." The coach threw the clipboard onto the seat behind Rusty and slung the cooler down the aisle, colliding it with Number 8's hindquarters.

"Hey!" she said. "That's my caboose!"

He told her he knew good and goddamn well what it was and to shut up about it and set the cooler on top of the spare tire while she was at it.

Turning back to Rusty, he said, "Why ain't we movin'?"

The bus door was still open, and rain spat in.

"Looks kind of bad, don't it?" he said. "Shouldn't we, um, wait it out?"

The coach leaned forward and removed Rusty's glasses. He called over Number 2, who was somehow remarkably drier than the others, and used her jersey to wipe off the lenses. As he placed them back onto Rusty's face, his fingers grazed Rusty's ears, sending a shock of gooseflesh down his back.

"You get us on home now," the coach said, using the same steady voice he'd used the week before when reciting a Miller Williams poem to Rusty's AP English class.

"Well," Rusty said. "Sure thing, Coach."

He woke up the engine, balancing his feet between the clutch and brake. The bus roared alive, two parts diesel, one part magic. He could feel it in his groin, the energy all throttled up. Before he let off the brake, the coach yelled, "Hey, Rus, you may want to close the damn door."

Door, yes. After it had been snapped shut, he shifted to first and guided the massive enterprise toward the road. The exhaust pipe popped off like a shotgun blast, the noise so deep he felt it in his molars. He was already on the interstate before he realized the sound had not been the bus backfiring at all, but thunder.

ONLY ABOUT FIVE FEET of road showed itself to Rusty at a time even with the headlights on bright. The rest was coated in murk. They were going along at forty, sometimes slower when approaching pockets of muddy water pooled in dips in the road. It was a solid two hours from home at a normal pace, but at this rate, it would be dinnertime before they rolled up to the high school.

Not that anyone on board seemed to mind. The Lady Tigers he eyed in the big circle mirror had donned headphones. Bone Thugs-N-Harmony's latest CD *E. 1999 Eternal* had been making the rounds on some of their Walkmans. To Rusty, their music was softer than what the girls normally listened to. Eerie lullabies more spirit than music, as if the singers were performing their melodies somewhere between the here and the hereafter. Two seats back, Numbers 12 and 8 sang along to parts of "Tha Crossroads," their voices not as ethereal as the original but just as mournful and loud enough for him to make out over the kerplunking rain and almost, *almost*, enjoy.

The coach lay on the seat behind him. Prime viewing in the rectangular mirror directly above Rusty when he leaned forward a little and cocked his head. A dangerous position, he knew, since it took his focus off the road, but he allowed himself a few glances anyhow. Not likely to have another chance like this one anytime soon: The coach had stripped down to his khaki shorts. He was dozing with his legs bridged across the aisle, his bare feet resting on the seat where his polo and socks had been draped to dry. He'd peeled his clothes from his pink and hairless body with a slowness Rusty had thought impossible in real time.

Lord, he said to himself, remembering it, and put his eyes back on the road. Wind was batting harder against the bus now. An invisible hand nudging them sideways. The coach had claimed the rain would slack up once they'd put some distance between themselves and the Delta. The god-awful Delta, he called it. Like with so many things, the coach had been wrong. The bus seemed bound for perdition, not away from it. Rusty believed in two versions of the coach: the one who taught literature to seniors and wrote poems for the school newspaper, *The Growl*, and the other one who was desperately over his head and had led the Lady Tigers to the end of a thankless season with no wins. During the era of Rusty's dad as coach, there had been trophies, special segments devoted to him and "his rowdy girls" on the local news channel, interested recruiters from as far away as Nashville and Hattiesburg. The Lady Tigers had been unbeatable their last season, state champions.

Rusty didn't like to wallow in thoughts about what went on last year, so he was glad when the coach came to and asked about their location. When he told him, the coach said, "My god, the Delta—it just goes on, don't it?" Before Rusty could respond, the coach nestled back into his napping position and closed his eyes.

Rusty tilted forward and stole another glance. The

coach was not much older than he was. Twenty-three or twenty-four. Fresh out of a nearby regional university with a teaching license. Rusty had been prepared to hate him out of some lingering loyalty to his dad. But his dislike evaporated during his first class with the coach, who came in reciting the famous soliloquy from *Macbeth*: "Tomorrow and tomorrow and tomorrow." Forney Culpepper—the name stuck in your throat. But otherwise he was beautiful. A boyish face, sandy hair he kept pushed behind his ears. According to *The Growl*, the coach was from the Delta, which maybe explained why he hated it so much, and a poet, which was what first drew Rusty's attention. According to Rusty's mom, who'd seen the coach milling about the Piggly Wiggly, he was also a lover of garbanzo beans and tofu. "Hippy-dippy shit," she called it, but not unkindly, for she wished him well, thank you very much, and didn't care who knew it.

Around the end of the first nine weeks of school, *The Growl* published one of the coach's poems. A sestina called "Hooch" about a dog killed by a couple's willful neglect of the animal. After reading it, Rusty bolted from study hall for the bathroom to wipe the wet from his face. He decided not to look at it a second time, though he could recite the repeating end words without even trying: *muscle, map, song, touch, trap, break*. Rusty mumbled them now as he plunged the bus deeper into a storm that showed no signs of letting up. He noticed the coach was changing positions, sitting up. He was scrutinizing the goings-on outside, and Rusty thought he was about to tell him to pull over. Instead, he placed a foot on the running handrail that separated the driver's seat from the passenger's. The foot was not in range of any of Rusty's mirrors, but he could picture it regardless. The smooth sole, the color of sunrise, relaxing against the chrome bar. The neat toenails, the instep, the delicate wrinkling of skin at the knuckles.

His eyes stayed ahead of him on the road, but he might as well have been turned around, ogling the foot, the naked foot, with his tongue hanging out like that woebegone dog in the coach's poem. Because he never saw it coming. Whatever *it* was—a chunk of asphalt, hail, god's own right fist? A diagonal crack slicing from the bottom left to the top right of the windshield was the only evidence it left behind of itself. After it ricocheted off, Rusty lost control and sent them careering off the road.

THE WEEK AFTER he had told his mom he liked boys, his dad confessed to inappropriate behavior with one of the Lady Tigers.

Rusty was stunned.

Not because it had happened, but because he had been around his dad and the Lady Tigers for years and hadn't suspected a thing. After he showed no talent for sports, Rusty was tasked with being his dad's lackey, going with him to all the games, keeping stats, pretending to care. His parents were worried about him, the way he did things like a girl, though that's not exactly how they put it. "Curious," they called it. When Rusty turned seventeen, his dad insisted he try earning a commercial driver's license and add chauffeur to his list of duties for the Lady Tiger's ball club. To his surprise, he passed both the written and driving portions of the test. So he spent his junior year carting the Lady Tigers around the state all while his dad had been sparking with one of them right under his nose.

Rusty had been distracted by his own secrets that year. His name was Robert, but everybody called him Sparse because he was so thin. He was black and wore glasses and had a tongue as red as a canary. When Sparse's parents found out about them, they sent him to live with an aunt in Memphis, and Rusty had been so depressed he confided in his mom, telling her everything. His mom said at first that she didn't believe in homosexuals. Rusty told her he was real enough all right, but they both knew what she meant. She suggested that they keep this between them.

So when Rusty's parents had called him into the living room one evening for a conversation, he assumed he knew the reason. His mom had caved. His dad knew. But no: He was all wrong. In fact, he probably couldn't be *more* wrong.

His mom did most of the talking. Very factual. The details: His dad had done this and this, and now this was going to happen. Rusty recognized the words but couldn't comprehend the language.

"Which one?"

Rusty's dad wouldn't say at first, and when he finally told him, the name meant little to Rusty. Because they were more pack than team and more team than individual people, he never bothered to learn their names.

"Who?"

Rusty's dad said, "The pitcher."

"Oh." He knew then. "Double zero."

"What?" His mom said. "*What did you say?*"

"It's not important."

She grabbed her purse and stormed outside. They heard the car pull out of the driveway into the street.

"She'll be back," Rusty's dad said.

Rusty had his doubts.

"Dad, right, so I'm gay."

"What? No. What?"

"Yeah."

"You sure?"

Rusty nodded.

"Hmmm." His dad walked into the kitchen and poured himself three fingers of Crown Royal.

The next morning Rusty found his mom on the couch,

dipping the ashes of her Virginia Slim into an empty can of Tab. "Your father," she said. "He's skedaddled."

"Where to?"

She didn't know, or if she did, she wasn't telling.

HIS GLASSES HAD BEEN knocked off, his shirt torn. His nose had taken the worst of it, smashing against the wheel. He remained semiconscious throughout. Conscious enough to realize the coach had been thrown into the stairwell. At first, the coach appeared more flustered than hurt. He clambered out of the entranceway and proceeded to call the Lady Tigers a bunch of bitches and Rusty a shit for a driver. Then his eyes rolled. His feet came out from under him, and he tumbled back down into the stairwell. The Lady Tigers rushed toward him, Number 12 barking orders to everyone else.

Meanwhile, Rusty tasted copper. Blood was eking from his nostrils into his lips. Without asking, Number 45 plugged his nose with tampons. When he tried to stand, Number 8 pushed him back down. She shined a small flashlight into his pupils and declared him to be concussed. He felt okay and tried to say so, but Number 8 said for him not to waste his breath—her mom was a nurse and she knew things, okay? His arms and legs worked. No cuts or bruises. Slowly, surely, the world settled down around him, and he began to understand a few things. For one, the bus rested at a slight angle, its grille buried in the gully of a ditch, the whole front end leaking smoke. For another, the Lady Tigers had divided into two groups. One to see about him, and the other to tend to the coach.

The sight of the shirtless coach being toted out of the stairwell by Numbers 12 and 2 reminded him of a painting. Christ being carried down from the cross. The artist and title of the work escaped him though it was a favorite of his. Just zipped out of his ear into the ether. Maybe he *was* concussed. They took the coach to the back of the bus and propped him up on the last seat. Because of the incline, they had trouble with his head—it kept drooping forward. Number 62 tried slapping him. When nothing happened, she did it again. Rusty got to his feet and lunged toward them. "What are y'all doing?" he wanted to know. Numbers 45 and 8 blocked the aisle. So he took to the seats, monkey-climbing from one to the other. The whole team swarmed him. Hands grasped at his clothes, and he twisted his body through the melee, pushing against the tangle of arms.

"Coach!" he cried, as Number 45 tackled him, knocking the tampons from his nose. After a mild struggle, she pinned him to the floor.

"I cannot breathe." Number 45's heft muffled the edge in his voice.

Number 12 said, "That's the point."

A slap of thunder rattled the window latches, and they all seemed to remember the storm outside. Number 2 wondered aloud if they'd ever see a sunny day again. Both Number 8 and 16 remembered passing a gas station a few miles back. One of them even recalled its name: the Space-Way. "Sounds like salvation to me," Number 12 said. A plan began to form. They'd wait out the weather, and as soon as it was clear, they'd backtrack to the Space-Way and phone for help. "911 and no fooling," Number 12 added. Number 62 worried about the coach looking so puny. She suggested another slap to rouse him. Number 8 disagreed, claimed she'd seen something on *20/20* about how violent people got if you woke them up from being knocked out. "That's sleepwalkers, dummy," Number 45 said, before asking Number 12 if she thought it was all right if she got up off the sissy. "My ass," she said, "is falling asleep."

"I second her proposal," Rusty said from beneath her.

Number 12 squatted and wanted to know if he was prepared to behave himself. He replied that he didn't see how he had much of a choice, being outnumbered and all. Which seemed good enough for her. She nodded, and Number 45 pushed off. He leaned up, the blood rushing back to his skull. He yawned so big that his jaws popped. Now closer to the coach, he noticed the knot on the man's forehead. The Lady Tigers regarded Rusty warily, as if he were a wild animal they weren't sure would bite or not, as he made his way over to the coach. Rusty rubbed his fingers across the swollen skin. The coach felt warm. Feverish.

"He looks so peaked," he said. "And we could be here a while."

"I'm open to suggestions." Number 12 crossed her arms.

He shook his head. "I'm fresh out."

"So did you just run us off the road for fun or what?" Number 45 asked.

"Or what," he told her.

Something like a smirk fixed itself on Number 12's face, and she told him to call her DeDe.

THIRTY MINUTES LATER, Number 45 spotted a funnel cloud and screeched. The other Lady Tigers scrambled up and pressed their faces to the windows, looking. Rusty and the coach remained where they were, the very last seats in the back of the bus, Rusty on the right seat and the coach on the left. The coach's head had tilted against his window, his breath fogging the glass, a dewdrop of spittle in the corner of his mouth. Rusty didn't like the look of the knot. All shiny, it seemed to grow bigger each time he eyed it. He looked away. He imagined they are still on the road, bound for home. He's driving and the coach is talking. Not the way he does around the Lady Tigers, but in that quiet, hungry way that falls over him when he considers poetry. "A genuine word eater," he once described himself, and Rusty tells the coach about Sparse. The time in the park, the time at his house after school. The way it burned the first time he touched himself after Sparse had been sent away. *Eat these words.* The coach, he understands. All too well, he says. The coach has known heartache too. Their eyes meet in the bus mirror—let's say the circular one. A hand finds Rusty's shoulder, squeezes.

The Lady Tigers hadn't moved for some time. Their faces were turned from him, on alert for cyclones outside. He tried speaking, *I am in a dream!,* but the words wouldn't come. The Lady Tigers turned as if they had heard him anyway. They turned and their mouths dropped open and they spoke with thunder.

He jumped awake.

Number 8 sat beside him, cussing. "You have a concussion, dumbass," she was saying. "No sleepy time for you."

"What about the coach?"

She told him the coach was a different matter but didn't bother to elaborate.

A greasy jar of peanut butter was making the rounds. The Lady Tigers used the same spoon to dig out a fat dollop and eat. Number 45 had opened the cooler and was passing out paper cups of whatever liquid was inside it—something purple. Seeing her reminded Rusty of the funnel cloud and he asked Number 8 about it.

"False alarm," she said, whispering. "She sometimes says things for attention."

DeDe, who was lounging in the seat in front of them, leaned over and told Number 8 she had an idea for how to keep the sissy awake. They'd tell stories, like around a campfire.

Number 45 trotted back down the aisle. "What kind of stories?"

"The kind with words," DeDe said, and everyone groaned.

Patting Rusty on the knee, Number 8 proclaimed she had one. "A real doozy," she said. "And it relates to our current predicament." She went on to describe this girl she knew in the first grade. "She had brown hair and was tiny, tiny. She rode horses and her parents were veterinarians." She snatched the jar of peanut butter and shoveled some brown goop in her mouth.

Number 16 gawked. "That ain't no story."

DeDe said, "And?"

Number 8 finished chewing and offered Rusty the jar. He declined.

Number 45 said, "What the fuck is even happening right now?"

As if that were her cue, Number 8 said, "Oh, yeah, a

tornado killed her." She paused, and when nobody said anything, she continued. "Well, not the tornado itself. See, she slept with her mouth open." She paused, and again, when nobody spoke, she added more. "So when the tornado ripped off her bedroom wall, her mouth filled up with all this, what do you call it, debris?"

DeDe interrupted her to ask the point of the story.

"Point?"

Rusty clarified: "Why are you telling us this?"

"I guess—I don't know—bad things can happen? Shit."

Number 16 grabbed the coach's limp hand and waved it at Number 8. "Hello, I think we know that already."

Even Rusty laughed while Number 8 waved her middle finger for all to see.

Number 62 said, "Coach Culpepper is the storyteller."

Rusty said, "He's a poet."

"Same difference."

DeDe told them to hush. She had one.

"Your nosebleed," she said, looking at Rusty. "Reminds me of Carrie-Anne."

Number 45 said, "Oh, jeez: the nosebleeds."

Rusty remembered. Nosebleeds had been her trademark. As she warmed up her throwing arm before a game, she sometimes got them. "Nerves," his father had called it. But they became the stuff of superstition. She was a force on the pitcher's mound anyway, lobbing balls past hitters twice her size. But during the games her nose oozed blood, she pitched perfect shutouts, not allowing a single player from the opposing team even a base hit.

Rusty said, "Double zero."

DeDe's eyes narrowed. "I saw her mama last month."

Number 16 said, "Thought they moved."

"Just to have the baby."

Rusty thought about the time he'd found them alone in the field house before a home game. His dad and Double Zero. He was holding a bag of ice to the bridge of her nose, trying to clot the bleed. He was up to his elbows in red, and the sight made Rusty feel sick. His dad should be more careful, he remembered thinking, letting her bleed all over him like that.

"I didn't know," he blurted out.

No one heard him: They were listening to DeDe. How she was in the Sunflower. How she was minding her own business, looking at crochet needles for her mom, when who rounded the corner? Carrie-Anne's mom, that's who. For a moment, a split second, DeDe considered hiding. "But I thought to myself: *No.* We didn't do nothing to be ashamed of, did we?" So they spoke. First about the weather. Then Carrie-Anne's mom said her girl was doing "just fine." Had earned her GED. Was taking classes at the community college. "And the shit of it is—she just pushed her cart on, went to the next aisle. Pretty as you please."

"I didn't know," Rusty repeated. "Promise."

Numbers 16 and 45 glanced his way. He couldn't make out their expressions. Something between pity and contempt. He didn't have the word for it, but he knew it well. It was the same look his mother gave him when he told her about Sparse.

"I used to drive by y'all's house after I found out." This was Number 8. She looked at her lap. "I used to think about driving my car into his bedroom."

"I used to think worse," said Number 45.

"Me too," said Number 16.

"I promise, I promise," Rusty was saying. He saw his mom dipping ashes in the soda can. She was telling him they'd be better off. With his dad gone. "It never happened," she'd said. "And I refuse to speak on it anymore."

Number 45 spoke up. "What I can't understand is why you kept driving us?"

Rusty nodded to the coach across the aisle, still unconscious. He wasn't sure if they understood what he meant until Number 8 said, "Figures."

"Her mom had the baby with her." DeDe was wiping her face. "Looks like you too. Same eyes."

"I promise," Rusty said again. "I promise, I promise."

DeDe reached toward him, and he violently jerked back. She was only placing a sweat rag against his nose. "Here," she said. "You're bleeding again."

THE LADY TIGERS STUCK to their plan. As soon as the weather cleared, some two hours after the wreck, they were trailing down the interstate toward the Space-Way. None of them wanted to stay behind with Rusty and the coach. Number 8 assured him they were both out of danger. Her mom was a doctor after all. When Rusty said he thought she was a nurse, Number 8 squinted. "Nurse practitioner," she said. He doubted very much that he was ever in danger, but the coach was a question mark. His knot still looked nasty. He came to when the girls were out of earshot and stumbled outside to puke in the ditch.

Rusty searched the front of the bus until he found the *Catwoman* comic wedged under the gas pedal. He looked it over: The raven-haired Selina Kyle had found herself in the jungles of South America, fighting drug lords with her usual mix of stealth, sass, and double-jointedness. The coach had put on his polo and was shoving his feet into his New Balances when Rusty stepped off the bus.

The weedy ditch felt soggy beneath Rusty's feet, a loud sucking sound with each step.

"I think they may try to fire me over this," the coach said. He stumbled to his knees when he tried to walk over to Rusty. The ground made more ugly noises as he straightened back up. "Second thought, I think I may just quit."

Rusty climbed the small bank and stood on the edge of the interstate. Bits of sunlight burned through the remaining overcast. Birds wheeled around in the big sky, crazed by the stillness left after the storm. Not a single car coming in either direction. That was the Delta for you: so empty it could convince you it was big. He rolled up the *Catwoman* and peered through it. The Lady Tigers were about half a mile away, toting their bats in case of trouble. But Rusty knew there wouldn't be any. They would probably confuse the hell out of whoever was working the Space-Way until DeDe explained everything. First to the Space-Way attendant, then to whomever she got on the pay phone. When Rusty got home tonight after being checked out by the hospital, he wouldn't begin with the wreck. He would cut to the quick: the baby. *Why didn't anybody tell me?* he would ask his mom. He tried imagining her answer, but none came.

"Rus?" The coach had managed to make it up the ditch somehow and stood beside him. "We got to think about what we're gonna tell them. What we're going to say."

Rusty kept looking at the Lady Tigers. The Delta was flat enough that he could watch them walking away for a long time. He dropped the comic and stretched out his palm. Like this, in forced perspective, he held the Lady Tigers in his hand.

"You wrecked us, but my ass is the one on the line, you see." The coach picked up the comic and swatted at Rusty's hip. "We need to be friends on this. Stick together. You know what I mean?"

Little by little, the Lady Tigers shrank. He regretted not learning all their names. Maybe there was still time. At school, around town. But he couldn't exactly picture them hanging out with him after this. *Carrie-Anne.* He knew that name. *Sister.* Well, he knew that one too. The coach kept on talking, and Rusty didn't listen to a word of it. He wanted to hold the team, all of them, in his palm for as long as he could, as they continued to get smaller and smaller until, at last, they were no more.

THE CURATOR

We're headed to the cemetery behind St. Peter's, to the gravesite of the Author. Even now, hordes of his devoted readers still pilgrimage to this little town in Mississippi and pay their respects at his grave. Many of them carry some form of dark liquor along with them, carefully placing the half-empty bottles of Wild Turkey and Maker's Mark around the enormous tombstone, the gesture a kind of offering to him, the Author, who had become, toward the end of his life, notorious for his drunken antics. Since we decided on making the trip at the last minute, however, we come empty-handed. No one remembers who suggested we come, but here we are, the four of us, off to see the Author, long dead these many years.

St. Peter's is a short walk from the bookstore; that is if you know the way to go. And we do. We've all lived here for some time. We cut diagonally across the town square, the dimly lit fronts of local department stores and cafés and pharmacies all hushed and empty at this hour, then we make our way down Old Timothy Street's cobbled pavement, passing the narrow Victorian houses with their large old-timey windows and low-ceilinged porches, and on up, farther still, we climb the little hill toward the First National Bank. Here, we take a left on Church Street where we can, at last, see St. Peter's steeple, a sharp, burnished needle pressing above the trees. On the tip of the steeple: a gold cross. From this distance, the cross appears delicate, vulnerable to the elements—almost as if a strong gust could come barreling through from the north at any moment and send the gleaming fixture cartwheeling across the heavens. I mention something like this to the others, but they ignore me. It's that kind of night.

We walk in pairs, two men following two women. The men are writers. One's successful, and one isn't. (I'm the unsuccessful one.) Ahead of us, the women stride arm in arm headlong into the dark, their slim bodies illumined by a fat moon. Grasshoppers sing softly beside us, invisible in the tall grass. The women speak in hushed voices like old friends, sisters even, and kick away pinecones that clutter about their ankles on the sidewalk. They are working things out between themselves, I know. One of them—the brunette—is married to the successful writer, and the other one (incidentally, I'm in love with this one) is sleeping with him. Everyone knows, of course: Tonight, there are hardly any secrets left among us worth telling one another.

THE AUTHOR WAS BORN a bastard in this town at the dawn of the last century, a time when Mississippi had started to regain some of the vitality it lost during the Civil War. The Author's town bustled with new life and optimism back then: The university had doubled in size since its founding fifty years before, and established families from Jackson and Natchez and as far away as Nashville settled around this growing seat of education, building grand houses in the style of Queen Anne Victorian, and none of them were grander than the Cartwright house. It was built a block and a half away from the town square, near Mr. Cartwright's pharmacy, and became somewhat famous for having the largest bay windows in the state.

A year before the Author's birth, the Episcopalians finished the construction of St. Peter's. The man who would become the Author's father, a rowdy steeplejack from Cincinnati, fastened the cross to the church's steeple sometime in the summer of 1898. That fall, a slight romance developed between Mr. Cartwright's daughter, a naïve debutante, and this selfsame steeplejack. Mr. Cartwright didn't think much of the match. He envisioned, like many fathers of that time and place and station in life, his daughter marrying a banker or a doctor or—at the very least—a pharmacist like him. Despite Mr. Cartwright's objections, the relationship continued, often in secret, and soon the girl found herself "with child," as they used to say back then.

Overwhelmed at the prospect of becoming a father, the steeplejack caught the first train to Texas. Some scholars conjecture that he worked the rest of his days in an oil field near Dallas, but that's pure speculation. In any event, no one heard from him again, and the Cartwright girl gave birth to the child out of wedlock, a great shame to her family. She didn't live long after, a rare case of toxicity setting in soon after the baby's first cries; the local newspaper called her death "merciful" and "proper" considering the circumstances. According to most of the Author's biographies, his grandparents, the austere Mr. and Mrs. Cartwright, treated him kindly, and he enjoyed a reasonably pleasant childhood with them, learning to read at an early age and spending most of his days, quiet and alone, prone in the expansive bay window of the Cartwright house, watching passersby and reading the likes of Hawthorne and Melville and—his favorite—Mr. Henry James.

By the time he was twenty, both of his grandparents had been entombed in the cemetery behind St. Peter's—where he himself would one day rest—and most of his other relations had scattered. Wayward and untethered to anyone or anything, he traipsed up and down the Eastern Seaboard before finally sneaking into Canada and joining the Canadian Expeditionary Force for the last year of the Great War. (The United States Army having soundly rejected him because of his flat feet.) After bravely fighting the kaiser, he spent the remaining years of his twenties in France.

During this time, his artistic inclinations seriously took root; here, in the City of Light, he transitioned from private journaling to penning brief vignettes about life in Mississippi. These were hard little gems of truth, his early work. He showed his writing to other American artists living there at the time, but they, as a whole, were not a very encouraging bunch and never accepted him into their ranks. Gertrude Stein, for example, found his accent too thick and cumbersome and his manners too boorish and his taste altogether questionable. "The man writes what he thinks he should write," she wrote in a letter, the one and only time she mentioned the Author by name, "instead of what he wants to write. He is, in a word, befuddled." His closest ally in France, a writer from the Middle West, advised him after a long night of drinking to return home and allow that setting—those people, their dark and funny ways—to nourish his creativity. The Author listened, and once back in Mississippi, he cloistered himself in the Cartwright house like a monk and wrote. Eventually, he published. His novels sold poorly and made little racket in the world, bewildering the finicky New York critics who deemed his style "experimental" and "cerebral" and his complex story lines completely "incomprehensible." Then, a year after his marriage to a woman who worked in the town's public library, the Swedes bestowed upon him an auspicious literary award, which garnered him almost instant international acclaim. The award surprised no one more than the Author himself. Now critics took a second, more thoughtful, look at his work, declaring him a "genius," and his reputation began to grow, as did his misanthropic tendencies.

BRADLEY HOLCOMB—he's the successful writer on our walk tonight.

Late thirties. A professor at the university in town. Popular among his students—especially the girls. Always dresses in some kind of flannel even in the summertime when the heat is so thick it has texture and personality. Because of his voluptuous eyebrows and protruding jaw, he appears, most of the time, to be brooding or deep in thought. He's from Virginia, and his accent, slight and noticeable only when he reads aloud, invites easy friendship and is not—as in my case, with my own muddy Delta twang—a joke. Earlier, before our walk to the cemetery, Holcomb read from his latest novel at a party in town celebrating its publication. The woman who's currently sleeping with him owns the bookstore that hosted the party.

Her name is Maggie.

Today, before Holcomb's reading at her bookstore, she confessed to loving him. I was there helping her and her small staff arrange things for the upcoming event; mostly, I was an extra hand to set up folding chairs and move tables and string up clear Christmas lights in the trees in the backyard. "It's sickening, the way I want him," she said, when we had finished the preparations and were having lunch alone in her office. I told her I understood, that I felt the same way about her. At this, she laughed, tilting her head back, exposing a white cream of skin under her chin. Physically, Maggie's remarkable: wild sprays of coppery hair, boyish hips, a face speckled with freckles, like a robin's egg. I've studied this face; I know it intimately. I know, for instance, that she rarely smiles because her teeth crowd and jut over one another in her small mouth, each tooth a slightly different shade of white. By all accounts, Maggie should be homely, but she's not. And on those rare moments when she does smile (or, as was the case at lunch, laugh), the effect on me is profound. Her provocative and unusual features—all co-opting together—turn her exotic, electric. How could you not love a woman like this?

After laughing at me for admitting my love, something

she'd known about for some time and chosen to ignore, she said flatly, "You're hopeless."

I said, "We both are."

She squinted. "Touché."

During the reading, I couldn't take my eyes off of her. She sat in the first row, her profile barely visible, and wept—a wet, gentle sort of weeping. Her tears glittered on her cheeks like liquid crystal, and I wanted to lick them from her face and then take her away from this place, from her bookstore and all these people who had gathered here tonight to honor the libertine writer Bradley Holcomb. Bradley Holcomb! He didn't deserve her. I sat behind the crowd of admirers, in the back with Holcomb's wife at my side. I met her for the first time that night. She clutched my arm the whole time her husband read. After he finished, Maggie, dabbing her eyes with a paper napkin, stood and led the crowd in an enthusiastic round of applause.

As the others around me clapped, I remained stock-still, and Holcomb's wife leaned over, and whispered, "That girl—she's really quite beautiful when in pain, no?"

AT THE URGING OF HIS EDITORS, the Author went to Europe to accept his big award from the Swedes, which came—he was delighted to learn—with a substantial cash prize. On returning to town, he sold his childhood home and bought thirty acres of land, mostly undeveloped, just south of the square. The spacious two-story house on the property was one of the few Greek Revivals not burned when General Andrew Jackson Smith went rampaging through the state, and came complete with servants' quarters and a horse stable and an outside kitchen. It's said that his wife, who came from humble means, had taken a shine to the place during her girlhood, and he bought the house for her as a belated wedding gift.

Not much is known about his marriage, but some biographers indicate that the relationship was somewhat tumultuous, even violent. He kept odd hours—a night owl who slept well into the afternoon—and he was known for talking to himself and making detailed outlines of his novels' plots on his bedroom walls with heavy charcoal sticks (he and his wife slept in separate bedrooms, another indication of their troubled life together).

Universities and libraries around the country called on him to speak, to give readings, but the Author rarely went. He preferred his privacy, working on his house and grounds instead. He lined his driveway with an alley of tall cedars and planted a large vegetable garden in the back and took a special pride, it was said, in tending to his only horse, an old Appaloosa named Bathsheba. His wife rarely ventured into town, and most of the townsfolk who interacted with her found her disagreeable, altogether too snobbish for the mechanic's daughter they knew her to be. Meanwhile, outside of town, around the country, a generation of emerging writers read his work, were inspired by it, and attempted to imitate the leafy Southern voice he had perfected in his prose.

However famous he became, the town always regarded the man as something of an oddity. Few in town read his stories and novels, and those who did were baffled or bored. They referred to him as, quite simply, the Author, and usually the utterance of this nickname was accompanied by an exaggerated eye roll or a huffy sigh. (Later, of course, his fans took to calling him the Author as a term of endearment.) Something happened between him and his wife a few years after he won the award, and the couple separated—although they never officially divorced. After his wife packed up and moved to New Orleans, he became a public nuisance. His relationship with the bottle became legend during this time in his life. Riding Bathsheba, he stalked the township at night and either yelled bleak obscenities or recited the poems of Keats and Wordsworth and Coleridge for all to hear. Years passed, and his behavior only worsened. The police arrested him on numerous occasions for public drunkenness and disturbing the peace. Some members of city hall talked about committing him to Whitfield, the sanitarium near Jackson, but before anything official could be done, the Author was caught in a flash flood one night and drowned. It was 1964.

After his death, the town and the university suffered through a hard time with integration and the civil rights movement and looked for ways to remedy its troubled public image. As they saw it, the Author, who had been buried there, represented an opportunity. They pooled their money, wrote grants, asked for donations, and bought his home from his wife and transformed the great house into a museum. The university, at the behest of the mayor, began holding weeklong conferences on the Author and his work every year in August, attracting scholars from around the world to their hamlet. And, in 1975, the board of trustees at the university commissioned an iron statue of him and erected it near the humanities department on the drill field. Often the recipient of bird scat, the statue, I'm assured by scholars, looks nothing like the real man: It's a thinner version with an amused face and a cocky stance, a pipe perched snugly between his smiling lips. The Author himself rarely smiled.

MAGGIE AND HOLCOMB knew each other for slightly more than a year before they started the affair. The way Maggie tells it, the wife—Gilly—knew about it almost from the start. "They are very open with their desires," Maggie told me. Adding, "Very French, if you ask me." Holcomb's attractive, in a rugged, sordid kind of way, so I understand the physical draw, but what moved Maggie to love him, or at least tell me she did, I can scarcely say. Her heart seemed so unyielding to me in this regard that I assumed all men were unlikely to snare her affections.

However irrational it may sound, I cared for Maggie almost immediately. Couldn't help myself. We met my second week in town. I had quit my job teaching high school after my first year proved disastrous and drove two hours east to settle here because I believed the atmosphere of the place, its "rich literary tradition," as the brochures called it, would be conducive to my desire to become, once and for all, a writer. Maggie was throwing a party at her bookstore—she's always throwing parties, it seems—this one was to commemorate the five-year anniversary of the bookstore's grand opening—and I was working part-time at the public library and had somehow been included in the invite with the rest of the employees.

I biked to her bookstore after work. Although I didn't know it at the time, the bookstore was in the old Cartwright house, the Author's childhood home. It was a prime location for such a store too, nestled between a popular bed-and-breakfast and a café renowned for its molasses pies. Two gauzy willows drooped on either side of the entrance, obscuring most of the house's beautiful frontage—including those lovely bay windows—from the street view. The heavy tangles of the willows pulled at my dress shirt as I stooped to pass under them and open the double front door to the glory inside.

Maggie often claimed she had refused countless requests from national magazines to do photo spreads of the interior of her bookstore when it first opened. When she bought it (at auction and presumably for a song), the house was all but condemned, the splintery walls and floors crumbling into themselves like stale bread. She completely gutted the inside and restored the rooms on the first floor to the appearances of an upper-class home of the late 1940s, furnishing them with stained-glass lamps, dark oak coffee tables, hard-cushioned couches with claw feet, and—in what must have once been the dining room—a baby grand piano, shining like a new car, side by side with an ancient and clattery cash register that Maggie insisted on using to do business. Each wall had a built-in floor-to-ceiling bookcase crowded with books—new and old, best seller and classic alike—shelved in no particular order. "Alphabetizing," she was wont to say to her customers, "kills the mystery. Let the book find you, darling." The second floor housed all the first editions and rare finds; she was more particular about these, keeping them behind glass cases under lock and key. The attic was Maggie's living area. "Not nearly as swank," she had assured me, though I had never been invited up there to see for myself.

The night of the anniversary party, I expected to be ignored by most of the people attending: boozy intellectuals who care more about what witty joke they can come up with than they do about meeting new people—least of all someone like me, a burned-out high school teacher/clumsy librarian/wannabe writer. Perhaps the crowd was more diverse than all that, and I simply wasn't in the mood to give them much of a chance to prove me wrong. The point is, there was free booze, so I helped myself to that and ignored the hell out of everybody else. By the time Maggie found me, I was squatting on the floor in a room that looked like it had once been a study or an office and was now the closest thing the bookstore had to a children's section. At some point in the night, though I can't recall when, I retrieved a glossy copy of *Goodnight Moon* and began to read it aloud to myself.

"You, sir," Maggie said, pointing her finger and drawing closer. "A birdy tells me you think you're a writer." Her words oozed out of her mouth in a slow assembly line of exaggerated syllables, and I was immediately glad to realize she was drunker than I was. Otherwise, I'd have been intimidated by her and the way she stood over me, swaying, her gray dress drifting up her long body like smoke. "It's in my blood," she told me, plucking the book from my hands and carefully sliding it back into the shelf above my head, "to foster and care for the likes of you." And she was dead serious. Before the night was over, she had introduced me to the current director of the board of trustees at the university, an easily romanced tree stump of a man. He was quick to inform me, after Maggie had left us to chat, that the curator of the Author's house had just retired and suggested I put in my application for the position, claiming if I was good enough for Maggie, then I was good enough for him.

A week later, they hired me—her word carried that much weight.

Like many small towns, this one had its bevy of local luminaries, and Maggie, only thirty, had established herself as one of the most notable. She claimed, I would later learn, to be a distant relation to the Author, purporting to be a member of his east Tennessee line—"a distant branch." Eager for anything concerning the Author, the town took her at her word (though some persnickety genealogists did express doubt) and began touting her as something of a living landmark. After its opening, her bookstore was added to the list of other official stops on the Great Author Tour, which was held every third Saturday and Sunday of the month. Her connection to her "Old Uncle," as she called him, bestowed upon her bookstore more panache than it would have otherwise garnered by itself even though it was already strategically located in the Author's childhood home, which helped to ensure—many believed, including me—its overwhelming success.

Her bloodline must give writers like Holcomb ideas about legacy and whatnot. I know because, well, it gives me the same ideas too.

AT SOME POINT DURING THE WALK, Holcomb laces his meaty arm into mine and begins to pontificate. Before tonight, we had never been in the same room; nevertheless, he seems intent on telling me the most private aspects about himself, like he's trying to stranglehold me into an intimacy he knows I want no part of. For some time, he goes on and on about the feeling that passes over him when he first wakes up in the morning. "Those bright few seconds," he is saying, "I lie there in my bed and am not myself. I am not Bradley Holcomb, but just—I don't know, you know?—pure animal, pure need. Need to piss. Need to fuck. Need to—to . . . *be*. Really incredible, and disheartening, when my ego clicks back into place and I remember who I am." Here, he pauses, gives me time to reflect, squeezes my arm. "You know what I mean?"

No, I tell him, I don't.

His face is splotchy. Which doesn't surprise me since he drank three glasses of scotch before we left the bookstore.

He asks me what I'm currently working on, and I tell him that it's a story about my gay uncle. Eyes wide, he says, "My god, aren't we all!" Then, perhaps now bored with me, he glances at the pair of women in front of us, their heads tilted together. "They're discussing us, you know," he says to me, winking.

His arm finds its way around my neck. "Can you feel them ahead of us?" he asks quietly. "Their warm bodies moving, the pumping of blood?"

My silence makes him laugh and prompts him to put me in an awkward headlock. "*Les belles dames sans merci*!" he says, and Maggie and Gilly stop and turn around.

In trying to remove his arm from around my neck, I unintentionally engage him in an impromptu wrestling match. We roughhouse in the street, both of us gasping and coughing like much older men.

"You'll hurt him," Maggie says, and I'm not sure if she's talking to me or Holcomb. Gilly, meanwhile, clicks her tongue disapprovingly, and says, "Gentlemen."

As if directed, he releases me, and somehow both of us lose our footing at the same time and tumble down the shallow ditch beside the road. The women laugh at us, the beautiful noise filling up the darkness. It's almost midnight, and the houses on this street are quiet and seem closed off to us, their occupants fast asleep by now, and the sound of Maggie's and Gilly's laughter must be apparent only to the lightest of sleepers, resonating on the outermost boundaries of their consciousness. On the wet ground, flat on my back, I imagine how both wonderful and sad it must be to have such a dream, a part of it true and never knowing about it.

Holcomb's the first to rise. Looking up at the women, he places his hand over his heart and closes his eyes. "I met a lady in the meads," he shouts. "Full beautiful—a faery's child, her hair was long, her foot was light, and her eyes were wild!"

Gilly steps to the edge of the ditch. "You shut that up—you'll wake the world."

"Aw, baby doll." Holcomb clambers up to the road and reaches for her, but she slaps him away. He shrugs and goes for Maggie, hoisting her over his shoulder and spinning her around and around. I scurry up the ditch and reach them about the time Holcomb and Maggie have stopped spinning and are, instead, kissing. On the mouth. Right in front of us.

I look at Gilly. "This is bullshit," I tell her. She smiles and shrugs, as if to say, *What can you do?*

Ignoring us, Maggie and Holcomb don mock-serious expressions and, gazing intently into each other's faces, appear to speak in a new way that doesn't require words. Then, coming to some agreement between themselves, they straighten their backs, clasp hands, and begin to dance. In fact, they tango—gleefully moving in the direction of the cemetery, Holcomb humming a Spanish lullaby along the way to keep them in step.

ON THE GREAT AUTHOR TOUR, the guides save the Death Trace for last. Here, visitors are treated to a small footpath that curves through the woods beside the Author's house to a low-level scrub of land near the river. In the dry summers, the ground is not much more than a circle of dust and red clay, but when the heavy rains come in spring and fall, the river spills into the woods and floods the Death Trace, turning the trail into a swampy pond.

Reports of what happened to the Author on the trace vary. Here's the one I believe: One stormy night in March, a loud clap of thunder spooked Bathsheba from her stable. Hearing her desperate whinnies as she trundled into the woods, the Author took off after her. The water had already reached his knees by the time he made it to the brush, but he kept on, sloshing down the path, calling out Bathsheba's name. He found the old girl tangled in the briar patch at the end of the trace. Her left hoof was broken clean off, and the river water was rising up around them at an alarming rate. He anchored down beside the beast in the muck, and together they faced the storm. The next day, after the waters had receded, his maid found them tangled around each other. No one knows exactly why he stayed with the horse. Scholars blame depression. Romantics, heartache and loneliness. Many in town say it's foolish to dwell on the motives of a drunk.

WHEN GILLY AND I catch up to them in the cemetery, they have transitioned from the tango to a spunky fox-trot around the Author's tombstone. The night's warm air feels denser among the graves, almost as if the mix of concrete and tombs and old bodies has congealed it. A few live oaks, with their swaying feathery tops, form a canopy and blot out the stars, leaving us, if it were not for a few nearby streetlamps, in complete darkness. Gilly and I sit cross-legged on the ground at the foot of the Author's grave. We have been defeated, the two of us, but Gilly seems more at ease with the loss than I do. She begins to sing, rocking her head back and forth, and the song is something French and sad. Maggie and Holcomb's dance slows, turns into something intimate and unbearable to watch.

"Why are we still here?"

Gilly stops midsong and taps me on the wrist. "She said I could have you if she could keep him for a little while longer."

I meet her eyes, and we laugh, her face mostly obscured in shadow.

"Don't I get a say?"

She kisses me. "Do you want one?"

I don't answer. Instead, we return to watching the couple as if they were characters in a play. Holcomb whispers something into Maggie's ear, and as she lifts her head to listen, the light from a streetlamp catches her face, and I see how, at that moment, she appears so achingly happy, the sheer brilliance of it nearly knocks me out. I know she's forever lost to me.

Bottles of whiskey and bourbon circle the base of the tombstone. Gilly gestures to them, and says, "My mother would find this behavior offensive." At first, I misunderstand and think she's referring to Holcomb and Maggie. "My mother wrote a book about the Author. She's the one who discovered his liquor of choice was Four Roses Bourbon." She waves her arms at the booze. "Not this down-market swill."

This talk frustrates me. She frustrates me, I realize, in a way I can't quite understand. So I nod to her husband, intent on picking a fight. "He seems pretty pleased with himself."

"Pleased?" She considers the word. She blinks and finally shakes her head. She snatches a clod of dirt and throws it at the tombstone, knocking over a bottle of Jim Beam. "Yes, he's pleased. Pleased to be here. Pleased with his book, yes. Pleased to have a wife who'll allow him to fuck just about anything he wants. But with himself? No—and there's the sadness of it all. With himself, he's never pleased."

She undoes her wasp's-nest tangle of hair, and blue-black curls suddenly fall about her shoulders, framing her face. "That urge," she says, "to create, to make something out of nothing—it's liable to trample over everything else. Best not to make a fuss. To let it pass on through."

I don't know what she's talking about. I tell her so.

"You write. You must know the feeling, the selfishness."

I shake my head.

"Ah, well, maybe you are not a real writer then. Maybe you are like me, one of those who likes the idea of being a writer but not the actual work of it."

"Oh, brother." I look above me to see if I can make out the steeple amid the network of branches and leaves, but it's not there. Like the stars, it's blocked. A few steps away, Maggie shifts herself in Holcomb's arms and bends over the tombstone. He's careful and almost tender as he pushes up her skirt with one hand and braces her slight body with the other.

I move to kiss Gilly, but she stops me. "The girl," she says hoarsely. "She doesn't see that Holcomb can't control himself. That he'll fly away. I'm worried for her."

"The fuck you say."

"No, really. He won't be good for her."

In front of us, Maggie holds on to the sides of the tombstone; Holcomb's fingers grip her shoulders, and his hips rise to meet hers. Then he settles himself deep inside her. Their moans start softly at first. Gilly moves closer to me but mumbles something to herself—a poem or perhaps a prayer. I'm not sure. She allows me to kiss her this time, and I push her flat to the ground and cover her body with my own.

AFTER THE AUTHOR'S DEATH, scholarship on him grew to an unprecedented, fevered pitch. He had many biographers, but none of them were as persistent as Dr. Lane Douglas. She grew up in a city on the West Coast, reading the Author's gothic tales of the Deep South. They consumed her. When finished with his novels and his collected and uncollected stories and the few vagrant poems here and there, she moved to the books about him and his work. Here, she hit a snag. The books, to her estimation, were unsatisfactory in scope and analysis—especially the material about his personal life. She had troubled over every word he'd ever written and felt these "scholars" had only glimpsed the artist—unlike them, she saw the man in full and was desperate to know even more: his favorite color, the way he made his bed. Everything.

She studied at good universities, earning a doctorate in

literature by the time she was twenty-five. Her dissertation on the Author's treatment of female characters in his early novels won her the respect of her committee and was published by a large university press. After an ill-fated dalliance with a fellow graduate student, which left her bloated with pregnancy, she took a tenure-track position at a small liberal arts college in New Orleans—not the best of options, to be sure, for someone with her qualifications, but she had her reasons for honing in on this place to live. Her next project would focus on the wife of the Author. This woman had lived the rest of her life in the Garden District after leaving him, and Dr. Douglas was determined to unearth the mysteries surrounding her, this strange librarian the Author had chosen to love. That would be her life's work—to understand the workings of the heart of one of the greatest artists of our time. Perhaps she believed her discoveries would alter the very bedrock of criticism surrounding the Author. Perhaps she thought that if she understood the type of person the Author had loved then she might know if he could have ever convinced himself to love someone like her. Eventually, Dr. Douglas gave birth to a screaming baby girl, a lump of warm skin that never inspired the maternal instinct, if such a thing exists, which Dr. Douglas strongly doubted.

As it turned out, the wife of the Author kept few records, rarely wrote letters, and made very little impression on the people in her neighborhood. Somehow, she had managed to fade out of existence without disturbing too much of the world around her, which must be recognized as a feat in itself. In the end, Dr. Douglas's dogged persistence turned up very little. A safe-deposit box was discovered, but it contained only some unimportant knickknacks: a silver dollar, some tattered gloves, and—perhaps most perplexing—a postcard from Sweden with the word *soon* written on the back of it in what was undoubtedly the Author's hand. After years of fruitless research, Dr. Douglas began, in her hopelessness, to hate New Orleans and the quaint college full of addle-brained students who braved to enroll in her classes, and—to some degree—she even began to hate her daughter, who was always there in the background of her mother's life needing something from her, something she couldn't wholly give without resentment.

Gilly says her mother went for many years like this, full of spite. Until, that is, a writer showed up one day at their door. Gilly was sixteen, and he was burly but articulate: a Virginian. He claimed that he'd read her mother's "insightful" book on the Author and realized that she, Gilly's mother, knew more about writing than any other person alive. He charmed them both, and her mother, it was no surprise, superimposed her obsessions with the Author onto him, this little upstart. She nurtured the young writer in every way: She gave him long, detailed notes on his writings and invited him to move into their small flat and, eventually, share her bed. "And we were a family," Gilly says. "For a while." But the problem with the happy years in a life is that they move by too quickly and rarely make it into the story proper.

When it became clear to the college that Dr. Douglas would not produce another book, they quietly asked her to leave, denying her tenure. About this time, one of Holcomb's stories was accepted for publication by a well-respected magazine. Within months, he was offered a job teaching creative writing at a university.

"Not just any university either," Gilly tells me. "But *his* university—the Author's. And Holcomb didn't ask us to tag along." Gilly and I are now alone, in my bedroom, the night after our trip to the cemetery. We stink of each other's bodies and need a hot bath. But she's telling me so much, opening up so freely, that I can't bring myself to move. She tells me about her mother as if she's been waiting her whole life to talk about her, as if I'm the one person in the world she has chosen to listen. "My mother became desperate again when he left," she says, and I rest my head in her lap.

Dr. Lane Douglas, failed scholar, jilted lover, had a new plan. She would write the book about the Author's wife anyway. What she didn't know, she would improvise, using her imagination, fabricating the sources here and there when called for. It took her a couple of months to finish it, and a small university press, lax in fact-checking, published it. At first, academia flocked to her book, dazzled by the wonderfully tragic story Dr. Douglas had crafted about the woman. The librarian and the Author were childhood sweethearts—in secret, of course, since the Cartwrights would never approve of his dating a mechanic's daughter. After his return from France, they married and tried to start a family. Several miscarriages later, the childless couple began, heartbreakingly, to turn on each other until the Author turned away and took to the bottle. Yes, it was high drama—and most of it completely untrue. A couple of weeks after the book's release, the first article was written to decry the falsehoods. In it, her book was spliced apart page by page for its "numerous and deliberate fallacies." A firestorm erupted, and the university press felt compelled to pulp the book. Academics denounced her; professors around the country took to calling her Dr. Lie. In an interview with Charlie Rose, she appeared intoxicated—which she was—and admitted to everything. Back in Mississippi, the town, wanting some of the publicity for themselves, called a press conference and banned her from ever stepping foot inside their city limits.

"Wait a minute," I ask, raising my head. "Is that even possible?"

"No matter—they put on a good show regardless, the damage was done."

Gilly's mother never recovered emotionally from the

vicious haranguing. Her drinking—Four Roses bourbon only, large bottles of it—increased. One night in December, she blacked out in a school playground, and by morning, she had caught a severe case of pneumonia, which eventually spread to both of her lungs. She died a few weeks later.

"Histories sound so much more depressing when you lay them out like this, end to end." Gilly nudges me from falling asleep, and I lift my head to kiss one of her hairy nipples. It's lighter outside my bedroom window, almost morning. Very soon, she will start putting on her clothes: first her underwear and her bra, then her pants and her dingy top. She will brush her hair, tie it into a loose knot. Finally, she'll tell me something that means, no matter what she says otherwise, goodbye. Goodbye and no more. But for now, she finishes her story. "Bradley came to her funeral. You should have seen him! All tears and blubber. You know how dramatic some Southerners can be. He practically proposed to me right there at her grave."

AFTER GILLY LEAVES ME that morning, there's silence in my life. Silence filled with repetition.

I go to work at the Author's house. Give guided tours of his beautiful home. I bike to my apartment in the evenings. I eat frozen Hot Pockets. I watch reality TV. I read. I write.

Maybe a sentence or two—nothing more. A month passes. Then two. Maggie finally calls me one morning.

"I need you," she says, "to come to the bookstore."

"What's the matter?"

"What do you think?"

DO YOU WONDER WHY we ever took to calling it *making love*?

I do. The term implies that with repeated and rhythmic penetrations we can somehow bring forth from ourselves the abstraction of what we mean to one another—call it *infatuation* or *lust* or, if you must, even *love*—and *make* this abstraction, transform it, into something tangible and concrete, some knot of magic that we can hold in our hands and show to one another, and say, "Look! This is it. We caught it." I guess some want, in the end, what we do to be special and different from what the malodorous hippos do, rutting themselves silly in a jungle river. Maybe for a few of us it is different. Maybe the lucky and the beautiful experience this love-made-solid thing I'm talking about every goddamn day of their lives. In my experience, however, people always leave the love that cannot hold them; they just slip right on through the abstractness of it all. The steeplejack left the debutante. The librarian left the Author.

The writer left the scholar. And now the married couple leaves the single misfits to fend for themselves.

Critics called Holcomb's new novel a masterwork. It was short-listed for every major literary award soon after the night of the reading. Then a private college in New England contacted him, offered Holcomb a lighter teaching load with a substantial salary increase. Gilly and he went to visit the campus and never came back.

Maggie says, "For days I thought about flying up there and finding them."

"And doing what?"

But she doesn't say, so we sit quietly on the back steps of the bookstore and drink Diet Coke and vodka, and listen to an old Nina Simone record. We are tired. We've spent all morning outside, stacking Holcomb's books into a great pile. Then we dosed them in kerosene. Maggie lit a match and tossed it on top of the books. Presently, we are watching them burn. Holcomb's books pop and sizzle, their gluey insides unfolding before us like bloated marshmallows. Smoke pillows around us, and Maggie raises her glass to the rising flames. "One day," she says, "you'll write about this summer." She's drunk—has been drunk ever since I came over. I gulp down my drink and tell her I may never write again. "Oh, you will," she says bitterly. "You're like him that way."

When the fire burns out, she leads me upstairs to her room above the bookstore. It's the afternoon, and light pools in from the windows, making strange patterns on the hardwood floor. We decide to close the blinds and shut the curtains. Still, the light ekes through and troubles us. We strip the comforter from her bed and duct-tape it over the windows. Now I can't see a thing. "Much better," I hear her say, and somehow in the darkness, she finds me, and we help each other undress. Then, all of a sudden, I hear sobbing. When she places a hand on my naked chest, I tremble and realize that it's me: I'm the one who's crying.

"This is what you want?" she says. "Isn't it?"

"Of course, of course."

In the long, bright afternoon, we cleave to each other, our sad, wet bodies, and I blurt out everything I can think to tell her—all my feelings, all my regrets. "Yes," she says, over and over. "Tell me, tell me." And once I start, I can't stop. I tell her how talented of a writer I am. I tell her how I want to be just like Holcomb only better, more successful. I tell her, my breath quickening, how I want to fuck his smell off of her. And Maggie—her thin body—can take it, every last bit, because she's not there, not really. She's eight hundred miles away, imagining the person in New England her body's pretending I am in the dark.

WHEN I GIVE TOURS of the Author's house, I always explain to the guests that many theories abound for why his wife left him, but this is what I believe to be true: She was second to his work. The whole trouble between them stemmed from that simple fact. After he won the big prize in Europe, she thought their relationship would change, deepen, mature; he would, at the very least, throw some attention her way. He didn't. Instead, he became more feverish in his desire to write—we know that he was working on three different projects at the time of his death. Like any talent, his was his greatest strength and his greatest weakness.

But what do I know? I'm just the curator.

I now stay late at his house, hours after the last guest signs the register and leaves. Maggie drives over in the evening. Our late nights have become ritual. We traipse over the velvet rope cording off the entrance to his bedroom. The twin mattress can barely hold the two of us. Around us, on the walls, his indelible charcoal etchings plot out the various lives of his characters, the words gleaming fiercely in the buttery light of the old-fashioned bulbs.

"It's all a lie," Maggie says once, running a finger along the dark marks. "I'm not really related to him."

"You're not?"

"Does it matter so much to you if I am?"

I pull her close, and the bed squeaks. "No, no—of course not."

She always leaves first after we finish—she never stays—

and later, I kill the lights to the old house and bike back to my apartment alone. On the way, I sometimes ride down the Death Trace. The trail's well-worn and easy to negotiate even at night. I pause at the bottom, where the Death Trace ends, and bellow out an old verse or two, something ornate, something I'm sure the Author would like to hear if he could. And the night swallows up my voice and spits back another, one that's all haggard from years of pipe smoke and hard living, so like how I imagine the Author's sounded. But, of course, this isn't really him. It's nothing more than a distorted echo, a trick of sound bouncing back to me through the trees—my desperate voice pleading to be heard by someone other than my own fool self.

THE LAST OF HIS KIND

It starts early one morning before sunrise. Someone hammering away at a rusty typewriter. Or perhaps hail: god-heavy, insistent. The three of them wake up nearly at the same instant and stumble from their rooms, half-asleep, blinking. At first, they act bewildered by the sound: Papa and his mother, MeMaw, and his son, Henry, believe someone's knocking at the front door. They shuffle downstairs, open said door to no one, and discover, instead, a woodpecker about the size of a softball needling at the house's awning at a breakneck pace. A miniature drill with feathers. Using a mop handle, Papa shoos the creature away. They almost laugh about it. Some kind of joke, they agree, before they climb up the stairs to their rooms—Henry wide-eyed, MeMaw complaining about her knees—and settle back into their beds.

Not an hour later the bird returns. The thwacking drives Papa from his bed first: He explodes out of his room this time, a firecracker, and stomps through the old farmhouse, shaking the floorboards. "Where's Dad's rifle?" he asks the walls. "What have y'all done with it?"

To Henry, his father's carrying-on reminds him of a thunderstorm, only closer and more personal. His room rattles with the sound of the man's anger. The chest of drawers facing his bed leaps toward him, as if alive, and tilts, almost turning over, before falling back into place. The door to MeMaw's room slams open. Henry rushes to his, which is closed, and listens for what may happen next. MeMaw hollers at Papa. She calls him a "shitass" and a "psychofuck" and a "sot drunk." She says he is acting a fool. His anger, she claims, has nothing to do with that pissy little bird and all to do with his wife who left him. "Delayed heartache," she tells him, grunting. "You may as well face it like a man. If you can."

Henry cracks open his door to find Papa looming over the old woman, his jaw tight. She doesn't move an inch under his glare, standing firm in her cottony nightshirt and her bare feet. She and her son have rowed many times before, Henry knows; each was used to the meanness of the other. Above them, the woodpecker keeps the racket going—a single pellet thrown at the same spot over and over.

"Gun," Papa says, in that fake calm voice Henry recognizes. "Where?"

MeMaw points in the direction of the boy. Henry shuts his door and sprints to his bed, hoping to bury himself in a pile of covers before the drama hurtling toward him now makes it to his room. Seconds later his father slaps open the door and flashes on the lights. Henry covers his eyes, keeps very still.

"Where? Where? Where?" Each time Papa shouts, his voice rises.

MeMaw trails behind him, breathing hard. She's become husky in her old age and isn't accustomed to moving so fast this early in the morning. She says, "The closet, you idiot."

Until then, Henry didn't know the rifle was in his room. MeMaw must have hidden it in his closet. His father's a poor shot, and his aim only worsens when he drinks. Which has been a fair amount nowadays. Henry also knows MeMaw makes it a hobby to hide things belonging to Papa and bide her time until he notices they are missing. She likes the power of knowing certain things, Henry figures, that her son does not—his papa, who thinks he understands the world better than the rest of them, she says, all because he's a writer.

"I'll be goddamned."

Henry opens his eyes in time to see Papa shoving out of the closet, rifle in hand. His face has become hard, something recently chiseled, and he looks as if he's about to point the barrel at MeMaw. Perhaps the thought crosses his mind, but he moves on, pushing past her. He carries the gun outside and fires some rounds into the darkness. A few sharp *kapows* punctuated by silence.

MeMaw has stayed behind in the boy's room, leaned over his chest of drawers, catching her breath. There's been enough excitement for one night. No need to follow him downstairs only to stir him up even more. Instead, she decides to wait until he has gone back to his room before she ventures back to hers. Henry's eyeballing her from his bed—that freckled face, that rowdy bush of red hair. Just like his mother. On her, at least, such traits were handsome. On the boy, bless him, they rendered him homely. Oh, he was some kind of ugly. And there is something else about him too. A differentness she can't as of yet place but knows that when it comes to a head it will endear him to few, if any, in this life. *Life has a way of crushing the special ones*, she often thinks. *Just look at what it did to me.*

"Go on back to sleep," she says. "It's over now."

They both know she's lying.

THE BIRD'S SCIENTIFIC NAME is *Campephilus principalis*. Also called the American ivory-billed woodpecker. Not to be confused with his Cuban cousin, which is much larger. Ornithologists have classified the ivory-billed as critically endangered, and many believe the species to be extinct since there hasn't been a sighting of one in nearly twenty years. Most of the time, these birds fly in pairs, mating for life. Like wolves and, occasionally, humans. This woodpecker hasn't found its mate, however—and won't because he is, in fact, the last of his kind.

Territorial and antisocial, the woodpecker once lived amid a network of decayed water oaks infested with black beetles and slugs, delicacies to the bird, but bulldozers destroyed his habitat the week before to make way for a new outlet mall. The bird traveled for two whole weeks throughout the Alabama clay fields and Mississippi floodplains before finding himself here, at this farmhouse, desperate for food. His wingspan of nearly thirty inches and the red-tipped crown atop his head make him an easy target for the man with the gun. But the woodpecker, nervy and suspicious by nature, is too quick for him. He easily disappears into the night when the shooting begins, unharmed. And he will be back, of course. Dense forest such as this is hard to find. Not to mention the roof of the farmhouse, alive with so many delicious termites.

HENRY'S EYES OPEN AT DAWN. Again to the sound.

Peck-peck-peck-peck during breakfast (a modest bowl of

Frosted Flakes) and *peck-peck-peck-peck* as he zips himself into a pair of coveralls and loads some paperbacks into his L.L. Bean book bag. The pecking's softer now, less frantic. Almost melodic, which probably explains why MeMaw and Papa are still asleep.

He leaves the house that morning to seek solace in a tree stand out in the woods. It's November, and most of the trail grass has turned gray and brittle, and cracks underneath his booted feet as he hikes to the stand, a small covered plywood box nailed securely into a thick pine. He often escapes there to do homework (he's homeschooled), but another urge sends him today. There's no danger of hunters lurking around; Papa's property has been posted for years, and many think he's too crazy and his land not worth the trouble to poach.

After he climbs into the stand, Henry sets down his book bag and retrieves a metal box from the far left corner of the squat room. Inside, he finds a scrap of paper he once tore from his father's senior annual: a black-and-white photograph of the varsity swimming team. They stand in a row—eight boys in all, not much older than he is. By the looks of it, the picture had been taken from a location slightly above the swimmers' heads. Someone must have perched on a ladder to get such an angle. Each of them gazes up with bristling confidence, their jawlines acutely defined. Wearing black Speedos. The gray-scaled pool behind them glistening. An illusion of undulation.

Henry props the picture against the box, then leans against the back wall of the tree stand. Positions himself. Unzips his coveralls and places a hand inside. He imagines them, the swimmers, battling the icy water with their lean muscly limbs. He stares at the photograph until his eyes are dry and he must, at last, blink. The swimmers look back at him all the while, smirking. As if they know the power their broad chests and smooth feet hold over him.

WHEN HENRY RETURNS HOME for lunch, Papa's outside in the backyard taking shots at empty bottles of Knob Creek and Four Roses set up along the creosote fence. He finds MeMaw prone on the couch in the living room, a damp cloth pressed over her eyes. "He's target practicing," she says. "Every two hours or so the bird starts up and your daddy goes nuts. He shoots and shoots. Hitting only air, the poor bastard." Between the bird and her son, MeMaw's not had a good morning, and she's come to an epiphany about her life. She has decided that all their troubles, the woodpecker included, can be traced back to her husband, dead and gone these forty years.

She leans up from the couch and takes the boy's hands into her own. "Now hear me out." She tries to keep her voice steady so the boy will take her seriously. More seriously than anyone in her life ever has. But she must hurry before they start up again outside. That pounding! That shooting! Her mind's liable to turn to scrambled eggs before it's all over with. "Founceroy Barfoot," she says, as if she were summoning him from across the room. "He's the one who done it to us."

The year was 1975, and MeMaw was pregnant and newly married and lived in town. Reuben Culpepper, her husband, and his younger brother, Lucas, had gone out one night to a bar called Fay's. "Which had been run by real-life hookers," she adds, but the boy looks unimpressed, so she continues on. She heard this story from Lucas, the brother, who was known to exaggerate, so who knows what really happened. But there must be specks of truth within it, she reasons. And some truth is better than none. The story went that Reuben won the deed to Barfoot's land in a game of blackjack, and Barfoot, a half-Choctaw, accused him of cheating. Barfoot chanted something, it was said, supposedly putting a hex on Reuben. Claimed no happiness would come to the Culpepper family. "And it has afflicted us all," MeMaw says, amazed at the words coming out of her mouth.

The boy pats her shoulder. She says, "We are cursed, baby. All of us." Age gives her words the illusion of wisdom, and she believes in them with all her heart.

Henry, on the other hand, is not as superstitious. Never believed in Santa Claus. God either. He does, though, believe in physics, nature's magic. What MeMaw has just told him triggers something in his brain that he remembers to be true. Something about energy. He has studied popular theories and has even come up with a few of his own. The way he sees it, there's good energy and bad. And energy begets energy, as everyone well knows. When his grandfather tricked old Barfoot (if indeed that is what happened), then he—his grandfather—set in motion a potent force of bad energy. Like a snowball tumbling down a mountainside, this bad energy kept on moving. Through his grandfather, through Papa, and now through him.

"We have to stop it," he says. Speaking more to himself than MeMaw.

Sometimes the old woman thinks the boy is as vacant as an air duct, but at other moments, like this one, when he seems so determined, she wonders if he perhaps understands everyone and everything with the profound sort of knowing befitting a mystic.

"How?" she says, trembling. "How?"

THE IDEA COMES TO HENRY at the public library: a letter of pardon.

While MeMaw busies herself in the stacks, he researches the Choctaw Nation online using a big clunky computer near the front desk that takes *forever* just to load a simple Wikipedia page. He first tries to find out about Native American curses but comes up short. (It wouldn't surprise him if *curses* are something the white man created; history shows them to be a mean race of people capable of all sorts of darkness.) One site did say the Choctaws once worshipped Hushtahli, the sun, and they believed nature to be ruled by a good spirit and a bad one. Maybe *spirit* and *energy*, Henry reasons, are different terms for the same force that's tormenting his family. Then he clicks on a link that takes him to the home page of the chief—a woman as it turns out. In the "About" section, it says how she's the first woman to be elected tribal chief. Using scrap paper, he jots down her address, and then, just for kicks, he googles Founceroy Barfoot.

Meanwhile, MeMaw wanders the nonfiction, looking for books on Morse code. For the moment, she's forgotten about Barfoot and her husband. She's noticed, instead, a pattern to the bird's pecking. And why the hell not? Most creatures in this world harness some means of communication. Bees secrete pheromones. Dolphins manipulate sound waves. You can even teach a chimpanzee sign language. Seems logical to her that a woodpecker would be no different. Evolution saw fit to bestow it with a sturdy beak, one that can be used for a multitude of purposes. The bird might very well be trying to tell them something. Tell *her* something. But the library's collection proves to have little on what she is looking for. A brief history of Morse code plus one thin children's book called *Morris Code*.

She finds the boy at a computer looking up stuff about the Choctaw Indians. On the way home, she tells him how the United States considered them to be one of the most civilized tribes in the country. Recounts for him how they even helped the Rebels during the Civil War.

"What about Barfoot? He's Choctaw," the boy says.

"Neither one had a good outcome," she tells him, her voice like the sound of falling gravel. "Your grandpa fell dead one hot summer day while shelling peas with your papa. And, not long after, Barfoot hung himself from a tree limb." On the particulars of Barfoot's death, MeMaw's memory is fuzzy. Something about it she couldn't quite recall.

Henry looks out the window as she speaks. Regardless of the details, he understands that in his neck of the world the air swooshes with a bad, bad spirit. He can feel it bone-deep, this energy. Age-old and prickly and sad. Everything is infected by it.

BACK HOME, Papa is shooting milk jugs. While MeMaw is in the shower, Henry sneaks into his father's closet and finds his old electric typewriter, a Selectric. He takes it to his bedroom and plugs it in. The typewriter hums to life. He needs the letter to be concise and direct—after all, the chief has a whole nation to run. To be better organized, he lists their problems, starting with the most direct.

Problem #1: the woodpecker.

Problem #2: his mother's gone.

Problem #3: his father and grandmother fighting.

Problem #4: his . . .

He can't bring words to this last one. He knows that he's different and has come to realize that this differentness in him must be in others too. Surely he's not alone in this. Logic demands there be others. Filters on the dinosaur computers at the library choke out the more interesting sites, and books aren't much help on the matter either. And he's not about to search the card catalogue for something he suspects to be in the restricted area. Or run the risk of the librarians getting wise to what he's looking for. No, no, thank you.

He's gazing at the keys, wondering what to type next, when Papa walks into Henry's bedroom. He asks Henry what he's doing with that old thing, nodding at the typewriter.

Thinking fast, Henry says, "I want to be a writer. Like you."

This is exactly the wrong thing to say. Henry knows it

the instant after he speaks. Papa laughs bitterly. He tells Henry to want in one hand and shit in the other. "Just see which one fills up faster," he says. He yanks the typewriter's cord from the wall and carries the Selectric back to his bedroom.

Times like these, Henry has to bite his tongue. Close his eyes. And breathe. Some days, it's all he can do not to set out on his own. Start walking and never look back.

He'll write that letter and mail it too. If it is the last thing he does.

And then: *the pecking*. There it goes again.

MEMAW'S IN THE SHOWER when the woodpecker starts up this time. Sometimes she thinks a bird lives inside of her, a small graceful thing aching to burst free and take to the sky. She grabs her breasts and squeezes them together. Allows the warm water to pelt her as she spins and spins under the nozzle.

THE WOODPECKER SKIRTS AROUND another flurry of shots. He flies deep into the woods, going from one tree to the next. Eventually landing on the tree stand, which is filled with the musky scent of the boy. A smell similar to the pit of a nest. Curious, he darts inside, scurries around some dry leaves, some sticks and dirt. Taps on a metal box with his knifelike beak. Then, bored, he moves on.

By morning, the woodpecker's back at the house, perched on the back deck. The boy comes outside and sits cross-legged on the ground and watches the bird. The bird watches back. The boy's smell wafts up around the animal. Invades the woodpecker's senses, overriding instinct. He hops off the ledge and moves closer on his toothpick legs toward the boy. The boy holds out his hand, and the bird alights onto his open palm.

Halito!

The purpose of this letter is to formally request a pardon on behalf of my family for an injustice we committed against one of yours many years ago. His name was Founceroy Barfoot, and the wrongdoing occurred sometime in 1975. We swindled him out of his land, which we still live on today.

The land hasn't been a working farm since my grandfather's time and, I assure you, isn't worth much now. Weeds clot the ground and strangle the trees. And the house my grandfather built is a mess: We stuff newspapers in holes in the walls to keep out the wind when it whistles through.

This pardon will be our first honest step toward something better. I've done some thinking and decided that if you want this paltry land delivered back to your nation I'm positive something can be worked out. One day, these acres will fall to me, and I assure you I don't want them. Not one square inch of them. When they're left to me, I'll sign them over to you. Gladly. You have my word, which I hope means something.

In the meantime, I await your pardon.
Yakoke,
Henry J. Culpepper

Out of the corner of her eye, MeMaw sees the boy slide an envelope underneath the pile of other letters to be mailed. When she takes the bundle to the mailbox across the road, she doesn't put the boy's letter in with the rest of them. Instead, she slides it into the folds of her extravagant muumuu. To read when she's alone.

Later that day, MeMaw rolls out an old record player from the hall closet and puts on George Jones. She and the boy square-dance in the living room for a time. "Orange Blossom Special" is her favorite tune; she can listen to that one all day long. Once, she was told that she had the voice of a bird. A bald-headed man named Bishop told her that.

He made her a lot of foolish claims though, and she believed every one of them. Followed that man to Nashville. Leaving her boy with some family in town. "I was too kind," says the old woman to the boy as they swirl about the room, "to be a star."

When they finish dancing, she tells him he can have one of her Miller High Lifes. They are at the bottom of the fridge: long gold cans, the champagne of beers. Henry cracks open one and takes a sip. He makes a face. MeMaw says, "You get used to the flavor."

She turns the record over, and George Jones's duet with Tammy Wynette, called "Golden Ring," fills up the house. MeMaw sings over the Wynette parts, her voice weak and achy. She imagines the little bird inside her being nudged awake. She sings and sings, her throat opening. She pictures the bird clawing up her rib cage one curved bone at a time, then, seeing light, flitting out of her mouth hole and soaring away. Oh, to be a bird! To shed this wrinkly skin and become all feather and claw. Nearly reptilian.

The boy, becoming braver, swigs the beer. Some of it fizzes down his chin, and MeMaw roars with delight. He wipes his face and comes in close, his face inches from hers, his eyes large and brown.

"I thought birds fly south for the winter. Why don't it fly south?"

MeMaw takes the boy's face in her hands and kisses it. "Because, baby, we *are* the South."

Henry laughs and falls back onto the couch. The world spins, and he decides to shut his eyes. Play like he's sleeping.

MeMaw's singing Dolly Parton when Papa comes downstairs.

"Shut that off," he says, and notices the boy on the couch, a can of beer still clutched in his hands. "You are the devil."

MeMaw shuffles some in her large tent of a gown. "Beer's good for the constitution," she says, and—thank god—her son snickers. Perhaps spending all his time focused on killing the woodpecker has drained him of some of his animosity toward her.

He takes a seat by Henry and palms one of the boy's bare feet. Though awake, Henry doesn't stir. The record has stopped, and the three of them sit quietly, a commingling of sighs. Both strange and wonderful, this silence among them, and Henry wants to hold on to it for as long as he can.

MeMaw breaks it by saying, "Our boy's like your daddy's brother was." Then a quick pop of another beer can opening. "He's in that way," she adds. Papa grips Henry's foot and says that Henry is too young to know what he is. "A woman knows," MeMaw says, and Papa coughs.

"There's no place for gentleness in this world," he tells her.

MeMaw winces at this. She feels the little bird inside her quiver with the truth of what he's saying. "Sometimes I think," she says, "that we are forgotten—out here, all alone—and it don't matter much what we do."

She takes the letter out of her dress and hands it over to her son, who accepts it without question.

Ignorant of this transaction, Henry, eyes closed, fights sleep, desperate to hear more of their talking, especially since it's about him. He wonders what they mean. *In that way.* But sleep wins, and he gives in to it so completely that he doesn't hear the woodpecker.

MeMaw jumps at the familiar sound.

"Going to let this one pass," her son says. "I'm tired of dealing with the damn thing."

WHEN HENRY OPENS HIS EYES, he notices that someone (probably Papa) has moved him to his bedroom. Outside, the ground is covered in a sheet of ice; the trees look frozen. The year's first frost. On the deck, he watches the purply sky turn pink with sunlight. That's the best part about living out here, he realizes: the sunlight—it touches everything when it gets going in earnest. The whole deck, white with frost, reflecting light. He sits in a plastic chair after scraping away some ice crystals.

Out of nowhere, the woodpecker flies down and lands on top of the little glass table beside him. This is not the first time that the bird has dared to come so close. Me-Maw's wind chimes twinkle. The bird's eyes look like tiny droplets of oil, and its beak, a tiny bone-colored blade. In books, he has read about boys and animals, how they form a connection, and then the animal most surely dies. And the boy then learns something about the harshness of the world. But Henry needs no such teaching. He knows the harshness better than most already. Knows his father will probably never love him like he needs. Knows his mother isn't coming back. Knows the pardon—how foolish he was!—will never appear in their empty mailbox. Knows too that a bird like this, so familiar with humans, isn't long for this world.

So he feels nothing when he snatches the woodpecker up and snaps his little neck between his thumb and forefinger: one swift breaking movement. There isn't any fight or tremble with the bird. Just acceptance.

There's no place for gentleness here.

Afterward, Henry notices that someone is screaming. It's MeMaw, who has seen the whole thing. She has collapsed in the doorway, her yawls gutting the sky.

PAPA INSTRUCTS HENRY to wrap the bird in a paper towel and meet him by his pickup truck. Henry does as he's told; in his hands, the bird's a bundle of sticks. When MeMaw quiets down, Papa comes out the side door carrying a small spade. He tosses it in the back of the truck bed, and says, "Get in."

They drive into the woods, to the tree stand, parking a few feet away from it. Papa digs a small hole in the icy ground. He waves Henry over. He's still holding on to the bird. Papa nods, and Henry understands: He drops the woodpecker into the pocket of exposed earth. Papa shovels it in, then knocks the spade against the tree, shaking off the remaining dirt clods. Looks up at the little box house some eight feet above ground. Carefully built. Still sturdy after all these years. "Read your letter," he tells Henry. "You need to watch MeMaw. She doesn't know the meaning of personal property."

Henry curses himself for his laziness in not walking the damn letter down to the mailbox himself.

"If you want to know the truth of it," he tells Henry, "then here it is. Right here." He gestures to the tree, the ground. "This, here, is where it happened. They said Barfoot hung himself, but most people knew what really happened. A group of drunks caught wind of his ways . . .

with men." Papa looks down, then back up at Henry, eye to eye. "You know what I mean, don't you?" Henry shakes his head: Yes, he does know. No point in lying now. "My uncle was the same way, but he was more quiet about it. More careful. Dad didn't steal land from Barfoot. Barfoot left it, you see, to Uncle Lucas." Papa goes on talking for a good thirty minutes, telling Henry about how his uncle Lucas built this tree stand and would wander out here at night before he died. "A kind of memorial," Papa says.

Henry touches the tree, feeling the crusty bark beneath his fingers. He glances above his head to the empty branches creaking in the wind.

"You understand me," Papa is saying, "what can happen to a person if he isn't careful?"

MEMAW IS SITTING in the recliner and thinking.

They have left her to bury the bird. "The boy," she says to the air. She clutches her arms, as if cold. That poor boy! Earlier, she heard him leave his room and go outside. She followed him and watched out the kitchen window as he murdered that bird. She knew that look on his face—that death glare—and yelled for him to stop before he ever put one finger on the bird, before he ever moved his arm even. And when he did what he did—lo! It was like he had reached a hand inside of her chest and snuffed out what little life she had left.

Now the bird inside her is in repose, mourning, half-dead with grief. It patters unevenly, and soon it will cease completely. She knows to keep this to herself lest they think her crazy, but she knows too that just because it's not really happening doesn't mean the bird in her chest is any less real. She thinks: *Forgive him, he knew not what he did!* And: *It's like I just woke up in this body. I am still that girl with big hair. I'm still singing. On the inside. It's the outside that went bad.* And finally: *My god, when did I get so old that I contemplated such deep things and quoted from the Bible. Goddamn it, fuck.* Me-Maw reaches for the beer can beside the recliner. Tips it over, and beer suds pool around her feet.

But no! It cannot end this way. Not yet. She will get up from this chair. In just another minute, when her chest settles. She will go to the phone and order them a pizza from the nearby truck stop—yes—and have it delivered before they return. They will gather around the table and feast tonight, the three of them. Start anew. She will cram her face with slice after slice of oily pepperoni goodness.

"Who'd have thought," she will tell her son, "that it would have been you and me together at the end?" Yes, yes: It will happen just this way.

"You two better appreciate me while you still can," she will tell the boys, *her* boys. "Tomorrow's never promised."

They will laugh at her. Forney will say, "Old woman, you'll outlive all of us." And MeMaw will shake her head and point to the boy, to sweet Henry. "That one there—he's the survivor in the family." Those words will be the truest ones anyone in this family, living or dead, has ever spoken; she will raise her beer can. "Henry James Culpepper, I bless you. I bless you with a long and happy life."

At this, Henry, smiling, will grab another slice of pizza and say, most assuredly, "Amen!"

Amen, amen, amen!

ACKNOWLEDGMENTS

This book of stories would not have existed without the following people (in alphabetical order): Lee K. Abbott, Jonis Agee, Joy Castro, Kathy Fagan, Michelle Herman, Lee Martin, Erin McGraw, Amelia Montes, Timothy Schaffert, Stacey Waite, and Nancy Zafris. Also, I am eternally grateful to the editors of various literary journals who first saw fit to publish these stories: the good people at *Day One*, *Indiana Review*, and *Third Coast*; David Lynn at the *Kenyon Review*; Meakin Armstrong at *Guernica*; Justin Taylor at the *Literary Review*; and David Yezzi at the *Hopkins Review*.

Many thanks to Noah Ballard, my tireless agent, and everyone at Curtis Brown, Ltd.

Kate Napolitano is my hero—now and always. Much love to everyone at Blue Rider Press and Penguin Random House, especially Emily Canders, Kayleigh George, and Caroline Payne, who had a hand in getting this book in order. All my love and gratitude to Katie Zaborsky, who was the fearless captain of this collection and led this book beautifully to shore.

Special props to the talented Tammy Carl for her artistry, and ditto to Cody Stuart for giving me the (cocktail) recipe for success.

Lastly, my family—thank you for letting me be me.